DEADLY CONSEQUENCES

Anthony Pathfinder

Firestorm Publications

Cover Design by Olga Francis

For more information, or to contact the author:

authoranthonypathfinder@gmail.com
www.anthonypathfinder.com

The cataloging-in-publication data is on file with the library of Congress.
ISBN: 9780615626093 (paperback)
ISBN: 9798838367716 (hardcover)

This book was printed in the United States of America.

TO THOSE WHO KNOW THAT SUCCESS IS A JOURNEY, AND NOT A DESTINATION

AUTHOR'S NOTE

I'm not an advocate of drugs, nor am I glorifying violence, quite the contrary. However, there are segments of our community where many of our young men and women are not dreaming the so-called "politically correct" dreams. They see themselves regulated to the bottom of the totem pole. Their view of the American Dream is not based on working a normal nine to five, but rather being the boss and calling the shots. Their dream is to get paid, right here and now, through the illicit drug trade.

The drug game has seen its share of drug lords whose commitment, dedication, determination desire, intelligence, and cold-blooded killer mentality have reaped tremendous wealth and bloodshed to achieve and maintain the lavish lifestyle and respect that comes with being a boss. Aware of the danger and luck that it takes to get ahead in the game, one must possess a combination of people's skills and intelligence.

The do-or-die mentality is more than a rallying cry for many; but rather a cultural and societal belief shared by those who feel that to attain their version of the American Dream, one must be fearless and ruthless. Along with their crews, bitches, nigga's, bling-bling, luxury cars and the frame of mind to get paid, their world and outlook are tied to the phrase by any means necessary.

My reason for writing this book is to depict the reality that so many of our youths are prone to get involved in. There is no doubt in my mind that a story such as this will spark the mind of some young man or woman. This book is about making choices, being responsible, and making decisions that will affect one's life. The examples and plight of the characters who are seeking to get "paid" will surely remind the reader of someone they know or knew; be it a relative or friend.

However, if my intention to shed light on this subject did not live up to the reader's expectations, then unfortunately I missed the point and I apologize. Come with me into the lives of these characters whose choices and Consequences will either be promising or Deadly.

EPISODE 1

Fuck that mutha-fucka! Black said to himself, glancing over his shoulder as he quickly opened the door to his mother's apartment. Tucked under his arm was a package. It was 1:00 a.m., in the morning. And knowing that his mother might still be awake, he tiptoed past the spotless living room, through the carpeted hallway, entered his bedroom, and tossed three brown paper bags filled with money onto his bed. He then reached for the black leather bag on top of his dresser next to a picture of his mother and younger sister. As he unzipped the bag, he emptied the contents of the package and began to count the crumpled hundred-dollar bills.

He walked to his closet, reached in, pushed aside several boxes of Reebok, Timberland, Polo boots, and sneakers, and reached for the one that was hidden in the back. Inside the old Nike sneaker box were two ounces of pure Colombian cocaine. An exciting rush of adrenalin shot to his brain as he sat on his bed admiring his small fortune, ten thousand dollars in cash along with Colombia's finest snow. He felt this was the start he needed, to establish himself in the drug game.

This is it! Now I'll be able to take care of Jasmine, Yvette, my mother, and my sister, he said to himself. Black and Yvette were the parents of Jasmine and despite their off-and-on relationship, he made every effort to try to provide for both of them. He and Yvette were high school sweethearts and after her pregnancy, their relationship soured. Despite it, they had a warm and close friendship. Black felt it was not only his obligation as a father to take care of his daughter, but he also felt it was the manly thing to do because his father was never there for him.

Although his stash paled in comparison to what most drug dealers usually start with, he figured he was well on his way to achieving his American Dream. He had every intention of doubling his money to make his first deal. This was how the young brothers from the "hood" survived.

The two brothers who came to mind were his close friends Divine and Trigga. They were new jacks in the game, and they were making a name for themselves. And Black figured; why not double his money with people whom he was familiar with? Not only did he admire the drug dealers and gangsters on his block, but he also knew he had to become familiar with them to establish his contacts and not get killed in the process.

Born in New York City to Jamaican parents, Black stood six-one, handsome with a muscular physique. He was a young man of perfect poise and presence. He was the epitome of the past, present, and future of the drug game. His cleanly shaven head embodied his mano a mano persona; bold, tenacious, sophisticated, and daring. His designer eyeglasses were perfectly perched on his nose. His dark skin was smooth and without blemishes or bumps. His nails were flawlessly impeccable: short, clean, filled. Black emitted an image of continuous physical perfection. In his presence, most people feel a certain aura of confidence exuding from him, but they sometimes missed the deadly glint that would flash in his dark brown eyes if they or someone pissed him off. Despite dropping out of high school, his intelligence level far exceeded most college graduates.

***

Twenty-three years old, and still living at home, Black was on a mission. For a moment, a chill of uneasiness came over him as he wondered about his partners Speedy and Riff. Earlier that night, they had paid a visit to the Polo Grounds Houses, a housing project at West One Hundred and Fifty-Fifth Street and Eighth Avenue. They had been shadowing Half Pint, the leader of the Get Paid Crew for quite some time. Half Pint, who got his name because he was short in stature, was always sensitive about his height. He and Black were never friends, despite knowing each other since middle school. Their dislike for each other was well known.

The Get Paid Crew, one of three rival groups fighting for control of the drug trade in the projects, had established itself as a cold-blooded organization that killed with impunity and Black was aware of it. He knew that Half-Pint and his crew were formidable opponents, but the element of surprise was what he hoped for. And when the time came, he struck like a poisonous snake with deadly force. He was precise and cautious to avoid any mistakes.

Half Pint had just picked up thirty grand from several of his workers and as he stepped off the elevator on the fifteenth floor, Black, Speedy, and Riff confronted him. Realizing he had made a mistake by not having his right-hand man Lil Jay with him, and staring in the nozzle of their weapons, Half Pint was defiant as he coldly stared at the men.

"What the fuck y'all niggas want?" he asked, barely able to control his shaking hands as they circled him. "Waddup with this shit, Black?"

He received an empty stare before Black responded. "What the fuck you mean waddup?" Black said, leaning in to get a closer look at his intended victim as he snatched Half Pint's Glock from his waistband.

"I thought we were cool?" Half Pint asked, with some uncertainty.

"Cool? We want the cake mutha-fucka, that's waddup!" Black snapped. Half Pint's dark brown eyes flashed with anger.

"It's like that, Black?"

"Yeah, it's like that!"

"Yo, Speedy," Half Pint called. "That's how y'all living?"

"Shut the fuck up and run the money before I clap your ass up," Black roared, pulling the hammer back on his weapon before Speedy could respond.

"A'ight," he said, holding the bags out. "Take the shit, it's cool."

"Bitch ass, mutha-fucka!" Black barked, snatching the money.

As Half Pint parted his lips to speak, Speedy smashed his fist in his face. Unable to see and with blood oozing from his wound, Riff ripped the two platinum-plated chains he wore around his neck and snatched his diamond-encrusted Rolex watch from his wrist. They began stomping him. Reeling from the onslaught of blows, Half Pint fell onto his side on the elevator floor, his face darkened with pain. His eyes widened with horror as his gaze darted back and forth across their faces.

Half Pint was certain he was about to meet his maker as the men dragged him into the fifteenth-floor stairwell. He had accepted his faith, and as he lay cowering, the men stared at him with disdain before coolly walking to the adjacent stairwell. Speedy, scrambling down the stairs ahead of Black, glanced over his shoulder and said, "Why didn't you smoke that mutha-fucka?"

"I know. I should have, right? Fuck it! Let's get the fuck outta here!" Black grimaced, scaling the stairs like an Olympic champion.

The trio bolted out the back door exit, ran towards One Hundred and Fifty-Fifth Street, and disappeared into the cool summer night. Several members from the Get Paid Crew were hanging out in the lobby of the building and the courtyard and never noticed a thing while their boss Half Pint lay bleeding a few floors away.

***

With his mind reeling back and forth and a small hope that his boys didn't do anything stupid like mention their good fortune to anyone, Black faintly heard the knock on his bedroom door. It was his mother. But his mind was on his uncle Joe, whose help he needed to get rid of the drugs. Joe, who was down on his luck and a low-budget street hustler still had a few links with several big-time hustlers in the Flatbush section of Brooklyn and White Plains Road in the Bronx.

"What is it, ma?" he asked, annoyed.

"Open the door boy!" she said, infuriated by the tone of his voice.

As she entered the room, he made a mad dash to hide the drugs and money under his bed. He hated his mother's snooping and the questions she would ask whenever he came home late. Seeing the look on her face, he tried to explain himself. Nonetheless, she didn't believe him and became more persistent when she saw a gun lying on the dresser.

"Oh, ma, it's for my protection," he said, picking it up and putting it in his closet.

She had a worried look on her face. Her eyes were watery. She asked in a concerned and sad voice, "Protection from what? The only people I know who carry guns are police officers and you're not one. Son, you have to stop living your life this way. I cannot take it anymore. Your father left me with you and your sister, and things have been difficult. I wish you would get your act together."

He sat on the edge of the bed listening. His shoulders were slumped, and his hands were clasped as she spoke. He loved his mother dearly and seeing that she was close to tears, he promised he would get a job and do the right thing. He hated seeing her upset. And knowing he was the cause of her anguish he made a vow that he would do things differently as the summer of 2004 took shape. No longer was he going to sit idly by like so many of the street corner drug dealers making pocket change. He was going to get in the game and get paid while making a name for himself. As soon as his mother left the room, he got on the phone and called his uncle.

"Yo, Joe!"

"Yeah, blood, why are you calling so late?" Joe asked sounding irritated.

"I've got some work. You think you could move it for me?" he asked, warily.

"That's no problem blood; I can make it work for you." Joe realized he could make a few dollars.

"I'm dead ass Joe-Joe, if you can't fuck with it just let me know."

"What I said? Didn't I say that I can move it?" Joe declared.

"Cool."

"So how is your mother?"

"She a'ight. She just left the room."

"She's giving you a hard time, huh?"

"You know how she gets sometimes," Black responded with some annoyance.

"Don't sweat it, man."

"I know."

"Cool but listen here."

"What?"

"I'll pick it up tomorrow."

"Thanks, Joe, later."

After hanging up the phone, Black jumped to his feet, and on tippy toes, he softly walked to his bedroom door; pressing his ear against it, he listened, but there was silence. He opened the door and began walking to the bathroom down the hall. He heard the clanging of pots and pans. Taking a peek, he saw his mother sitting at the kitchen table lost in her thoughts as a pot of water boiled on the stove. Any inkling he had of her eavesdropping on his conversation was quickly dismissed.

"What you doing, ma?" he asked, in a cheerful tone.

"I'm making some tea, want some?" she asked teasingly, knowing that he didn't like tea.

"Nah. You know I don't drink that stuff," he said, walking to the bathroom.

"Make sure you put the seat down," she hollered.

"I will ma," he said, hoping she would hurry up and go to bed.

Jennifer Reynolds was forty-five years old and of slight stature. She stood five-four with a light complexion and big innocent brown eyes. A hard-working Harlemite, she left the Caribbean Island of Jamaica for a better life at a young age.

As faith would have it, she met a suave and charming William Reynolds on the subway on her way home from The Borough of Manhattan Community College. Immediately attracted to his good looks, and a fellow Jamaican as well, they began dating, which eventually led to marriage and two wonderful children. Dropping out of college to become a housewife and mother, led to a lot of financial woes; and the marriage began falling apart.

It also didn't help that Mr. Reynolds was an excessive drinker and womanizer. It wasn't long before he walked out on the family. Although they never legally separated or got a divorce, because their financial situation prevented either of them from doing so, Mrs. Reynolds refused to seek the government's help. She got a job at Harlem Hospital as a nurse's aide. She was hardly ever home. She worked a lot of overtime to provide a better life for herself and her children.

EPISODE 2

It was 10:00 a.m. when Black's cell phone rang. On the other end of the line was Cory Baxter, known to his friends as Speedy. Dark brown in complexion, tall, with curly hair, and a known ladies' man, Speedy was the player in the crew. Friends since elementary school, he was very loyal to Black and like him, had dropped out of high school.

"Waddup, son?" Black asked.

"Yo, come by my crib, we got some shit lined up. We about to get paid!" Speedy said, in an ecstatic tone.

"Word? Gimme a minute, a'ight."

"No doubt, later."

When Black arrived at the apartment, sitting in the living room were Speedy and Suzy, a close friend of theirs. Witty, eccentric, with a sense of humor and clowning most of the time, Suzy was known in the neighborhood as a small-time hustler and stick-up kid. Half Dominican and half African American, Speedy, Suzy, and Black became fast friends as classmates at Public School 23, in Harlem.

As a kid, Suzy would watch the repeats of the television series "Happy Days." His favorite song from the series was "Wake up Little Susie," which he would always sing, hence the nickname. He never liked the name or the spelling while growing up. But after years of being called by the name, it grew on him.

"Waddup, son?" Black asked, hugging both men.

"Chillin'," they both replied.

"Where you been, Suzy?" Black asked, plopping himself on the couch. "This is our first time seeing you in like two weeks right, son?"

"No doubt," Speedy answered, nodding his head.

"I've been busy working on some shit that's about to blow up," Suzy told them.

"For real? So, let's hear it," Black said, sitting up on the edge of the couch.

"Check this out. I know this cat that is making crazy loot in the game," Suzy said, staring at both men. "He's into this shit big time, bro. I'm not talking about that street corner bootleg bullshit. Son, this dude is moving mad keys."

"Word? Where you get all this info? And what's the brotha's name?" Black asked, curiously.

"Hold on. Im'a get to that. Son got Spanish Harlem on lock, and check this: he hitting them outta state, too. Yo, he gets paid. You name it; he got it, Beemers, Mercedes, and Jaguars. Son is living large," Suzy smiled.

"We still don't know his name," Black said irritated, wanting to know more.

"The mutha-fucka's name is, Choco."

"Does it sound familiar?" Black asked, looking at Speedy.

"Nah."

"Same here son," Black shot back, getting up from the couch.

"What I wanna know is how do we go about hitting a cat like that?" Speedy asked.

"Yo, I got it all figured out," Suzy grinned. "My cousin hangs out with him all the time."

"Your, cuz? Who is that?" Speedy asked, glancing over at Black.

"Maria," Suzy answered shaking his head at how Speedy asked the question.

"Why the fuck are you shaking your head? What? We supposed to know who the fuck she is? Who the fuck is she? Memo to Suzy, her name doesn't ring a bell. We've known you for years and I ain't never heard you mention her before, have you, Speedy?" Black asked.

"Nah, son."

"Fuck y'all. I'm trying to tell y'all how we can get paid and all y'all wanna do is give me a hard time, fuck that! Y'all, think I got to tell y'all about everybody in my family?" Suzy smirked, totally frustrated.

"Why the fuck you o'd'ing son?" Black laughed.

"Chill Black, let me explain," Suzy quipped.

"What does she do for him?" Black continued, with a huge grin on his face.

"It ain't like that. She hustles with him. You know what I'm saying?"

"Oh, yeah?" Black asked, sarcastically.

"Don't even try it, son. I know what she's about."

"Hmm, finish what you were saying playa," Black continued.

"Son, dude is a coke head. Homey be sniffing that shit twenty-four seven. And y'all know that's the cardinal sin; never get high on your own supply. We could get paid. Every time he sniffs that shit, all he wanna do is fuck, drink, and sleep and that's where we come in." He said it excitedly.

"What the fuck do you mean by that? That's where we come in?" Black asked, getting serious.

"Slow down Black, damn! He hangs out a lot in Jimmy's Manhattan Café. It's a Dominican night spot," Suzy went on.

"A'ight, I know that joint," Black responded.

"Y'all with me so far?"

"Yeah, son!" both men said.

"She's gonna get his ass twisted and roll with him to his crib."

"Then what?" Speedy smiled, knowing the answer.

"She's gonna let him hit it and then crash. He won't know what the fuck is going on," Suzy said, giving the men a weary look.

"She's gonna give up the pussy? So, I was right! You see what I'm saying, Speedy? Why is this nigga frontin'?" Black laughed aloud.

"Yeah, son, why you frontin' about that shit?" Speedy added, laughing.

"This is business," Suzy snapped.

"A'ight, since you say its business then that's what it is," Black replied, urging him on. "Like I was saying right, once he's out, she's gonna let us in and boom, we do what we gotta do. And just to make sure that shit goes right, Im'a give her some jacked-up 'caine mixed with rat poison and all that other shit," Suzy disclosed to the men.

"What the fuck? For what?" Speedy snapped with a surprised look on his face.

"In case he wants to sniff once he's back in the crib. Fuck that! I ain't taking no chances that mutha-fucka is dangerous, son. I'm covering all the bases. Trust me, yo, if he needs that shit, she'll give it to him and set his ass straight."

"I'm listening," both men responded.

"Once it's in his system, we roll up in that bitch and do him."

"And you saying your cuz is willing to do this?" Black asked wanting to be one hundred percent sure.

"Hell, yeah! She's with it."

"So, she's gonna fuck him and do all that other shit, and then we do him?" Black asked warily.

"Yeah, once he gets the pussy along with the jacked-up 'caine, it's a rap!" Suzy snickered.

"Just like that?" Black smiled.

"Yeah, just like that!"

"How does this sound to you, Speedy? 'Cause I'm saying, why we can't just do this mutha-fucka instead of going through all this," Black questioned as Speedy considered what he said.

Before Speedy could respond, Suzy added, "I don't know. I ain't feeling it like that, fam. Maria says once this cat is fucked up, we can take him. When he's sober, he's no joke and I know y'all don't wanna fuck with that nigga when he's sober because I don't."

Despite Choco's reputation as a cold-blooded killer, his behavior was erratic, and as dangerous as he was, he had a weakness for alcohol, cocaine, and women. This was known to only those closest to him and Maria was a part of that close-knit group. And although no one from the group had ever tried to pull off such an act, Maria was willing to take that chance. If the plot to rob him was to go through as planned, Maria knew she would be the prime suspect. But she wasn't discouraged; she and Suzy agreed they would relocate to another state if the job was a success. Black thought it was a great idea.

"Hmm, what do you think, Speeds?" Black asked.

"It sounds cool to me."

"And like I said all we have to do is roll up in that bitch and we paid," Suzy said eagerly waiting for Black to respond.

Speedy was the first to commit to the job. "Okay, I'm in and you better be right about this shit, son," Black added, glaring at Suzy as he thought about adding several grand to his stash.

EPISODE 3

Maria grew up fascinated by the thug lifestyle and the fast money allure associated with the drug game. She was street smart and knew the game. Along with her cousin Mercedes, Suzy's younger sister, they were runners for several of Harlem's most notorious drug dealers. The only thing that mattered to her was getting paid. She knew that money ruled the world, and she wanted her share of it. So, sucking a dick or two, or sleeping around to get what she wanted, never really bothered her. She felt as long as she used a condom, everything was fine. Despite her outlook, she once attended Stuyvesant high, an elite public school in Manhattan on an academic scholarship.

Maria stood five-six, with a dark mahogany complexion. She had dreamy eyes and a small nose with slightly flared nostrils. Her lips were full and soft. Her striking jawbone betrayed her Taino ancestry. Her face was beautiful to look at. Her breasts were firm and full, and her long legs were perfectly suited for her shapely figure. She was the second of five children born to Carlos and Sylvia Alou in Spanish Harlem. Growing up, her family was on public assistance like many families from the ghetto. As a source of income, her mom Sylvia did a few baby-sitting jobs in the building where they lived. Her father Carlos never held a steady job. He drifted from one job to another. Sylvia and Carlos argued and fought constantly, and Maria was no stranger to any of this.

It was a hot summer night and Carlos was gambling in the local neighborhood after-hours gambling spot. He was drinking and checking out some of the fine women who held his attention with their explicit gyration and flirtatious behavior when he was fatally shot after getting into an argument with one of his buddies over five dollars.

The Alou's world was shattered upon his death. Maria became a woman overnight, as things quickly changed for the family. Her mother was now dependent on her more so than ever. She became the woman of the house. She kept a watchful eye on her younger siblings, especially Cheena, who had caught the eyes of several of the neighborhood drug dealers.

Maria's mother struggled to provide for her family and her older brother Ernesto helped out whenever he could. Ernesto was involved in a lot of illegal activities and got into far too many confrontations with the police. It finally caught up to him and on his seventeenth birthday, he was convicted of manslaughter and armed robbery.

To make ends meet, Sylvia invited a host of men into her home. A typical night at Sylvia's apartment was filled with alcohol, drugs, and sex. Sometimes the men stayed and helped the family, but they always ended up leaving. They were sleaze-balls and were only looking for a place to shack up and to get some pussy. It wasn't long before Maria started doing sexual favors for money with several of the neighborhood drug dealers. They took care of her financially and in the process, she learned the game.

It was while attending Stuyvesant high school that things began to unravel in Maria's life. Along with Mercedes, they started hanging out with several high rollers from the lower East side of Manhattan. They had stepped up their game and were making a lot of money. They drove around Harlem in the latest luxury cars and SUVs. They flossed in the hottest fashion and bling.

It was during this period that Maria dropped out of high school. She didn't give a damn. She was doing things her way and could care less what others thought. Days, weeks, and months would go by without a word from Maria, and her family became worried, especially her mother, who feared for her life. On any given day or weekend, Maria delivered several kilos of cocaine and crack between Pennsylvania, Rhode Island, and Delaware.

The job was becoming more and more dangerous as the Feds intensified their surveillance at the airports and train stations and had arrested several people who were being used as drug mules. Maria, like other females in the business, became more creative. The drugs were compressed into small amounts and then put in balloons. She would swallow as many as she could or insert them into her private parts. Once the drug was skillfully hidden in her body cavities, the only thing she had to worry about was her composure once she approached airport security.

This was her greatest fear and in the drug game, things can go awry in a matter of seconds. Yet, she took it all in stride. She lived for the moment and the adrenalin rush she would get, knowing she was outwitting the Feds. She took risks and rose above them while avoiding jail. As far as Maria was concerned, this was her job. And like any other worker, she was putting in her work. It had also helped when her drug-dealing associates increased their cash payments to their airport and train connections.

***

Things didn't turn out as well for Mercedes as they did for Maria, so she decided to get out of the game after nearly getting killed. El Loco, a Colombian crew from Jackson Heights, Queens, kidnapped her late one night as she delivered a package. The crew had the house under surveillance. They knew who the runners were and the day the drop would be made. The Colombians targeted Mercedes because she was an easy target. They had considered hitting the drug house but decided against it after noticing Mercedes' frequent visits. They knew Mercedes would be alone the night they approached her.

"Where's the rest of the drugs?" one of the four men demanded, in a thick Colombian accent.

"This is all I have," Mercedes whimpered. She was scared as she begged for her life.

"Bitch don't lie! We have been watching you for a long time now. We not stupid, where's the rest of the drugs?" the man asked angrily.

"You won't hurt me, right?" Mercedes pleaded.

"No. All we want is the rest of the drugs," the man smiled.

"Okay," she said handing him the package she had in her bag.

"We know there's more. Where's the rest of it?" he barked at her.

She began unzipping her pants when he said, "Oh! That's where you got it, mama?"

She barely uttered, "Yeah."

"We don't want you to take it out here. We take you to somewhere else," the man said, admiring her body.

"You promise you'll let me go, right?" she asked, in a scared and nervous tone.

"Si mami! I tell you before we only want the drugs," he reassured her.

The men drove her to an apartment in the Elmhurst section of Queens.

"Where is the bathroom?" Mercedes asked terrified.

"No, no, no bathroom. Take it out right here," the man said as his partners smiled. Their eyes were glued to her body as she pulled her pants down, displaying a pair of French-cut panties.

"Go ahead," the man doing most of the talking said.

She pulled her panties down; they slithered off her hips showing her rich milky complexion and shaven pussy. She inserted her fingers inside her vagina. Their eyes were wide open as she pulled several balloons from her vagina. She then bent over and stuck her finger in her ass, straining as if she was having a bowel movement, and several neatly laced balloons fell out of her ass.

"That's it," she said in a shaky voice.

One of the men then walked over to her and grabbed her pussy with such force that she fell to her knees crying, "Please don't do this!"

"We won't do nada. We let you go now," he said, as he slowly loosened his grasp on her pussy.

After taking the drugs, they beat and raped her repeatedly inside the apartment. When they were done, they put her in the trunk of their car, drove to the West Farm section of the Bronx, and dumped her almost lifeless body. She was never the same after that near-death experience. She walked away from the drug game to be with her two children.

***

Upon hearing the news, Maria was even more cautious than she had ever been. Yet she didn't let it stop her, as she continued working her ass off. It was through a mutual drug-dealing friend that she met Choco. They became fast friends, and it wasn't long before he offered her a job. Working with him had its ups and downs, but she stayed with him. She was making decent money, but it paled in comparison to what he was making and that bothered her. She thought about running off with several small shipments of cash and cocaine but remained loyal. It was only when he decided to cut her pay that she became outraged. She normally made two thousand per delivery and it was cut in half. She was furious because so many people depended on her. It was then that she decided to turn on him, and with the added pressure from Suzy, she finally gave in.

***

Black was curious as he thought about Maria and the role that she would play in them pulling off the robbery. He had committed several small-time robberies himself, along with his buddies; but never with a female, and one who was playing such an important role. This troubled him deeply and after talking it over with Speedy; he called Suzy and told him he wanted to meet Maria.

Black couldn't keep his eyes off her the day they met. She was as beautiful as Suzy described her. Speedy was also taken by her beauty. Realizing this, Black quickly approached her and introduced himself. They had a brief conversation before deciding that they would meet up in two days. It was business as usual at their next meeting. And after going over all the details, they agreed that the time was right to make their move. Suzy reminded Maria to take the spiked package of cocaine he had given her the day before.

She hopped in a cab and headed downtown to One Hundred and Sixteenth Street and Amsterdam Avenue, where she met Choco at Jimmy's Manhattan Café. Jimmy's was happening as usual. The place was filled, and the crowd was partying. It wasn't long before they decided to leave. They arrived at his apartment sometime after 3:00 am. Black, Speedy, and Suzy waited anxiously in Riff's car for Maria's phone call. Riff was born in Jamaica and came to New York as a child. Unpretentious and shy, he was handsome and stood a slender five-eleven. He and Black met each other in elementary school, and like Speedy, he was loyal to him as well.

"Suzy, we're at the crib," Maria said in a whisper, unaware that Suzy had her on speaker phone. Black and Speedy smiled as they listened.

"How is he? Is he fucked up?" Suzy asked.

"Yeah, but he's still up. I think I'm gonna have to work on him," Maria informed him.

"A'ight, but don't forget to use the 'caine if shit ain't right."

"Bet. I'll get back to you, okay," Maria assured him.

"A'ight."

Their adrenalin was sky high as the jitters overcame them. An hour passed and nothing. They were worried that things may have taken a turn for the worst and Choco wasn't going to comply. They were about to call it quits when Suzy's cell phone rang, it was Maria.

"I gave him the 'caine. He's doing it," she said.

"A'ight, let him go ahead," Suzy replied, thrilled.

"I'm scared Suzy, suppose the shit doesn't work? What if it kills him?" she asked nervously.

"Chill out Maria, don't be saying shit like that!" he told her, trying to calm her down.

"Okay, but…"

"But what?"

Sensing that something was wrong, Black snatched the phone from Suzy.

"He wants me to suck him off," Black heard her say.

Black responded, "It's not like you've never done it before." He didn't know why he said it, knowing he was attracted to her.

"Please!" Maria said realizing it was him. "And why are you on the phone, Black?"

"Come on now, Maria, we are about to get new money. Now is not the time to be fucking around," he snapped, visibly upset.

"But damn, you ain't had to come out your face like that!"

"My bad, you right. Just do your thing. I'm sorry okay."

"Okay, give me some more time."

"Take all the time you need. We'll be waiting," he smiled, hearing the calmness in her voice.

"Okay, bye."

As Choco snorted the cocaine, Maria unzipped his pants and took his semi-hard dick in her mouth. She slowly ran her tongue over the head of his dick and began sucking it. Holding her by the head with one hand, Choco snorted the remaining cocaine as he shoved his dick down her throat almost choking her.

"Sniff some more," Maria suggested in a sexy and seductive voice, taking an air break from the dick.

"Caramba!" Choco yelled.

"You like it, papi?" Maria asked, removing her clothes.

"Yeaaah!" Choco moaned in a trance-like state.

Maria then got on top of him and began working her pussy on his now hard dick. He was banging her pussy like a man possessed.

Damn! What's taking this nigga so long? I wish he would hurry up, Maria grumbled to herself.

"Shit! I'm gonna cum!" he yelled out.

"Yes, baby! Come on! Let it out! Oh yes, papi!" she moaned, hoping her words would get him off. Her words worked wonders as he exploded.

Finally! Maria thought as she waited for him to fall asleep.

***

It wasn't long before he passed out. He had no idea that Maria had let the men inside the apartment.

"Damn! Son, this shit is fly!" Speedy said, upon entering the apartment.

"Yeah, this mutha-fucka is living large," Black smiled.

Within minutes, Choco was bound and gagged.

"Why the fuck did you tie him up, Speedy?" Suzy complained.

Before Speedy could respond Black interjected, "Fuck that! So, what if he's out of it? I'm not taking any chances. You did say that, right? Well, I'm doing the same thing."

"Yo, if he wakes up and sees that he's tied up. He's gonna know it was Maria. What's up with that?" Suzy argued.

"Yo don't worry about it son. With his money, we can go anywhere and chill. Let's do this! You the one who had the mutha-fucka doped up," Black snapped.

Maria who hadn't said a word had a somber look on her face as Black playfully winked at her. They frantically began searching the apartment. They found a few hundred dollars and several packets of cocaine.

"This can't be it, is it?" Speedy said to no one in particular. Things weren't looking up as frustration began setting in.

"The closet, check the closet and the flooring," Maria said.

"Are you sure?" Black asked.

"Hell, yeah, I'm sure. There's gotta be some shit in here."

They headed to the bedroom and began ripping apart the bedroom closet. They removed the flooring inside the closet where they found ten kilos of cocaine and one-hundred-and-fifty grand buried under the boards. Suzy began ranting and raving to the others about getting out of the apartment.

"Yo let's break the fuck outta here! This looks like it!" he shouted.

"This is it?" a concerned Black asked, glancing over at Maria with a look of disbelief on his face.

"Why are you acting like that?" Maria questioned him.

"What do you mean, why I'm acting like that? Is this it or what? Let me know!" he asked, with a baffled look on his face.

"Nah, it can't be, he's got more shit trust me. Check his pants pockets!" Maria said. She wasn't about to give in that easily and neither was Black. Black searched his pants pocket and found his car keys.

"What color is his car?" Black asked.

"It's a black Lexus SUV," she replied.

Black and Suzy headed downstairs to check the car. Hidden inside the rear of the Lexus was a green military-style duffel bag.

"Jackpot!" Suzy said, excitedly.

With wary eyes, Black paid particular attention to the small group of people he saw walking up on down the block before coolly tossing the duffel bag over his shoulder as he and Suzy headed upstairs. Once inside the apartment, he opened the duffel bag and tossed its content onto the living room floor. They were all astonished to see the amount of cash and Colombian cocaine that fell onto the carpet. They were in disbelief as they looked at each other in amazement.

"Oh, shit! This mutha-fucka was driving around with all this shit in his whip? Unfucking believable! What the fuck!!" Speedy said, shaking his head.

Their hearts were racing. They were taking quick breaths and the palms of their hands were sweaty. The enormity of what they had pulled off was slowly creeping in.

"Speedy, go see what's up with that nigga," Black said.

"Yo, Black, he ain't breathing!" Speedy yelled.

"Word?" He was shocked.

"Son, he's dead!" a grim-faced Speedy responded.

"Let me take a look. Damn! This mutha-fucka is dead!" Black uttered with a look of incredulous disbelief.

"Oh, fuck! Let's get the fuck outta here!" Maria began crying.

"Relax, Maria; we have to clean the place up, okay. Once everything is straight, we'll bounce, a'ight. We ain't leaving nothin' for the po-po," Black said in an authoritative tone while telling Suzy to put the drugs and money in the duffel bag.

"But he's dead, Black!" Maria stated nervously.

"I told y'all not to tie him up," Suzy countered.

"Suzy, save that shit, a'ight! Shut the fuck up! Everybody has to remain calm. Okay, he's dead. But there's nothin' we can do about that. So don't get shit twisted. Let's finish what we came here to do," Black said, pissed! They were getting on his nerves.

"No doubt! You right," Speedy said as he and the others began wiping their prints from the apartment.

***

Spanish Harlem was on heightened alert the next day, as the news of Choco's death hit the wire. The rumor machines were working overtime as the innuendos and varied scenarios concerning Choco's death hit the playgrounds, crack houses, street corners, and barbershops. The police immediately launched an investigation, but virtually ran into a brick wall of silence. The no snitching code of the street reassured Black that he had nothing to worry about. His only concern was reprisal from Choco's friends.

Aware of this, he and the others kept a low profile. When they finally resurfaced months later, they split five hundred and fifty thousand dollars in cash and twenty-two keys of cocaine four ways. Black gave Riff his cut from his share. The businessman that he is, he quickly suggested they start their organization. He knew Suzy and Maria would have a difficult time getting rid of their stash, which wouldn't be the case for him, Speedy, and Riff. It was unlikely that Maria would continue doing business with Choco's connection for fear of reprisal. As for Suzy, he would bring a lot of unwanted attention to himself, which would eventually lead back to Black, if he weren't controlled; and Black feared this happening.

"I'm talking big-time people and we just have to be smart about it. I'm talking about the biggest supplier in Harlem and the other boroughs, bigger than Bumpy Johnson, Frank Lucas, and Nicky Barnes," an unsmiling Black spoke with a lot of fervor.

"Who the fuck are those people?" Suzy asked.

"Those cats use to run Harlem back in the day," Speedy said nodding his head.

"I never heard of them," Suzy said.

"They were real gangstas son, word, right, Black?" Speedy added.

"Hell, yeah, they were real gangstas. School 'em," Black uttered.

"Damn, Suzy, you don't know shit," Speedy laughed.

"Check this out y'all; look at some of the cats that are running shit in Harlem? Those mutha-fuckas are soft, and if those poo-put-doo-doo-scoopers who ain't shit can do it, why can't we?" Black asked waiting for an answer.

"I'm feeling you, son. Half Pint and them cats from the Polo Grounds are doing the same shit. We gotta get in the game like those cats," Speedy said.

"That's exactly what I'm talking about, Speedy. We can set up shop right here. I know a few cats that are willing to supply us, including our homeys Trigga and Divine," Black stated.

Black was straightforward and didn't give a damn what others thought about him. He wasn't your average brother from the "hood." He was a voracious reader. He read a lot of books on Japanese and Chinese culture. He also read the poetry of Kahlil Gibran. He embraced the idea of authenticity rooted in the philosophy of "death before dishonor" and the significance behind "the sword is only as powerful as its master." He knew that to get paid, he had to have a plan. And he knew that anybody in this country, who is somebody, had a plan. And it's a plan they believe is worth dying for.

"Every mutha-fucka that ever got paid in this bitch had a plan," he continued.

"No doubt, Black, 'cause all them cats like the Rockefellers, Kennedys and Hearst's they were robbing mutha-fuckas left and right," Speedy added, as he eagerly awaited his response.

"That's what I'm talking about, that's what's up! We have to follow those cats' blueprint. They had a plan to get paid, and that's exactly what they did," Black emphasized while making his point.

"Word!" Speedy said interrupting him.

"Whether you do your shit legit or not, the only thing that matters is your mutha-fucking plan. Without it, the shit is a waste of time. You gotta have a plan and you gotta stick with that shit and deal with the consequences, good or bad," Black continued.

"I'm listening," Suzy kept repeating as Black stared at him and the others.

They were listening intently to Black when he asked, "What are you planning to do with your share of the money, other than to spend it all in one place? What? You gonna go out and buy the fly rides, hook your mom's up and then blow the rest of your gwop?"

"Nah, that shit doesn't sound cool," a supportive Speedy added.

"Speedy, will you be quiet!" Maria said, gesturing for Black to continue. Black loved that.

"Listen, if you jerk all your money, are you gonna put your life on the line again for a measly couple of grand when you just got paid big time? We can easily invest the shit we got left over, easily doubling or tripling it. The only thing that matters to me is getting paid. Because a mutha-fucka will try to set you once he sees you shining. And your gwop better be long, to deal with that shit. And you better have an expensive mouthpiece when the po-po rolls. You got to be able to make bail and to take a snitch out."

"Yo, the shit is real, Black," Speedy said undaunted by the looks from the others.

"But the thing is we can't afford to bring too much attention to our shit. We have to be discreet as possible. We can't settle for that street corner, penny-pinching, five-and-dime bullshit. You know, the shit where a bunch of mutha-fuckas is just hanging and holding up the block. That's played out, y'all. We don't need that. And remember, trust no one but each other," he made clear to them.

"For real, Black," the others said.

"This is deep, Black! Choco never said anything like this. I mean he did say some shit, but that was it. But this, this is on point," Maria exclaimed with a slight smile.

"I hear you, Maria, but now you rolling with a brotha who doesn't want any mistakes. In this game, mistakes are not an option. I'm a hustler. You are a hustler. We all hustlers till we die. We ain't nothin' more and nothing less," Black spoke confidently.

"I hear that," she said.

"So, what are we gonna do? Are we gonna do this or what?" he asked the group.

Speedy and Riff were immediately sold on the idea. Maria was somewhat apprehensive, but after hearing everything that Black had to say, she changed her mind. Suzy was also pessimistic but, with a little persuasion from Maria and Speedy, he agreed.

Black was an odd combination of intelligence, confidence, egocentrism, paranoia, insecurity, bravado, and swagger. He felt the circumstances that led to his getting paid were the ticket to living the American dream and embracing the gangster lifestyle, which would put him at the top of the drug world.

EPISODE 4

Three months later . . .

Black knew Maria was attracted to him from the moment they met and although she pretended as if she didn't, he knew better. She had listened intently to him and how he explained things not only to her but to the others as well about laying low and keeping their mouths shut. Maria also saw the respect that he had earned from some of the neighborhood's most notorious drug dealers. For someone who was just getting into the game, he had a lot of admirers and Maria respected that. She also liked the fact that he was a take-charge type of guy, which she mentioned to him on several occasions. Aware of this, Black offered her a ride home after one of their meetings.

"Sure," Maria said taking a seat in his Jaguar.

"Where to?"

"The Bronx. I gotta get my ride from my cousin, Mercedes."

"Sure, no problem. I was wondering what happened when I saw you rolling in Suzy's ride."

"It's a long story, but Suzy wouldn't let his sister hold his ride to go shopping. So, I let her use mine."

"That was cool. It says a lot about you and the type of person you are. I bet you are the concerned type, aren't you?" Black smiled.

"I guess, but what do you mean?" she said gazing at him.

"You know, dependable, someone you can count on, a person with a heart of gold. It's refreshing because a lot of people would have said no as Suzy did," he said, touching her legs. They both laughed. Their eyes met momentarily.

"Thanks." The friendly tension between them heightened.

Black felt this was an opportunity he couldn't squander, as he drove across the Macombs Dam Bridge into the Bronx. Maria was dressed in a pair of tight-fitting Parasuco jeans with a matching top. His heart was racing as he stared at her. *Damn, she's beautiful,* he said to himself. Nonetheless, he had some questions he wanted to be answered.

"Do you have a man?" he asked, nervously.

"No, and no, I don't have any kids. I knew that was coming next so I figured I would answer it for you," she giggled.

"You sure?" he asked smiling. "Are you . . .?"

"What, seeing anybody? No, I'm not," she replied, cutting him off. She smiled while trying to avoid his eyes.

"You better keep your eyes on the road," she said shyly.

"It's difficult keeping my eyes on the road and you at the same time." He smiled at her.

"That's why I'm telling you to keep your eyes off me," she teased.

"Why should I?"

"I don't know," she said, blushing like a ten-year-old about to get her first kiss.

As he pulled up to the red light at the intersection of One hundred and Forty-Ninth Street and Third Avenue, he reached over and kissed her. She reciprocated as they began tonguing each other down. If it weren't for the honking car horns, they would have continued kissing.

"What you wanna do, ma?" Black asked biting his bottom lip as he stared into her gorgeous eyes.

"Whatever you wanna do," she replied taking a glance at him and then looking straight ahead. He opened her zipper and began rubbing her pussy with his right hand. She lifted her ass some making it easier for him to slide his finger through the side of her panties and penetrate her moist pussy. She reached for his dick and began jerking it back and forth. The temperature inside the car was overwhelming and unbearable, as he sped on the Bronx River Parkway. *Damn, I should try to beat some of this traffic and see if I can make it to the Renaissance Hotel, in New Rochelle,* he thought to himself. But he thought better of it, seeing how the Parkway was backed up and exited at Boston Road. He sped towards the Quiet Storm Motel, which was on Boston Road. He was excited, as he pulled into the parking lot of the motel. And as they were getting out of the car, Maria said, "You need to do something about that hard-on."

"Like what?" he asked sheepishly smiling.

"You can't go in there like that," she said laughing.

"Why not?"

"Because it's showing that's why. Damn, it's big!"

"I got it," he said, laughing as he pulled his shirt over his bulging crotch. He quickly paid the motel fee and playfully urged Maria toward the room. Within seconds, they were undressed.

"Damn, baby! You got a beautiful body," Black drooled as she walked over to him naked and began kissing him. He was lost in the moment as he sucked and licked her swollen tits.

"Oh, yes! Right there, Black!" He slowly worked his way down to her wet pussy and began eating her out.

"You like this?" he said smothering his face in her moistness once again.

She moved her hips to the movement of his tongue and as it darted in and out of her, she grabbed his head. Her hips were moving faster and faster as she felt an orgasm coming.

"Oh, Black! Yes, baby! Just like that!" she yelled as her cum absorbed his freshly cut goatee.

"You taste good," he muttered.

"Lay on your back," she told him, taking his throbbing manhood in her mouth. She ran her tongue down the side of his bulging shaft. He moaned as she deep-throated his dick. He grabbed the pillow and placed it over his face, muffling his sounds. She drove him wild.

"No more, no more!" he begged as she playfully bit the head of his dick. She was sucking the life out of his manhood. His eyes were focused on her face as she took his shaft and his balls in her mouth.

"Oh, fuck! You're gonna make me cum!" he yelled.

"Okay! I'll stop! Let me sit on your dick now."

She straddled his dick and began riding it.

Black was like a man possessed. He met her rhythm and began banging her.

"Oh, God! Don't stop, baby!" she squealed. She was in ecstasy. She closed her eyes and began to slow wine on his dick. He was hitting the pussy doggy style as she tried to pull away from the powerful strokes, he was laying on her.

"Are you mad at the pussy?" Maria asked looking over her shoulder at him.

"Yeah, uh, yeah, uh," were the only words he could muster.

"So, what are you waiting for? Show me that you're mad! Fuck me! Fuck me, baby!" she moaned biting her bottom lip.

He yelled out moving in and out of her love tunnel at a frantic pace before exploding.

Exhausted and thrilled, he was beside himself as he stared at her sweaty body. He couldn't control himself as he stuck his tongue down her throat. As he lay there, he wanted to tell her how awesome the sex was but decided against it.

***

2005 started great for Black and Maria. They were spending a lot of time together. They partied at the hottest nightclubs and dined at the finest restaurants. It wasn't long before he asked her to move into his Manhattan condo. Suzy didn't like the idea and made it known to Maria. He knew Black's reputation as a player and that bothered him. Black was visibly upset when Maria told him what Suzy said and quickly confronted him.

"Yo, Im'a say this one time and one time only, don't ever disrespect me, underestimate me or challenge me. I don't give a fuck if you are Maria's cousin. I will fucking merk you! Do you hear me?"

"I got you. I fucked up!" Suzy stammered nervously.

Suzy kept his word and never mentioned or questioned Maria about her and Black's relationship. Maria and Black were in love, and that was the end of it.

***

Days later . . .

Black was cruising around town, something that he loved to do when his phone rang.

"What's up, baby?" he answered hearing Yvette's sexy voice.

"I thought you were coming by?"

"I am. I'm on the ave. I'll be there in a few."

"Don't play with me, Dante."

"I'm not; I'm coming, give me a minute."

He showed up as promised. He greeted her and Jasmine with a hug and kiss.

"I thought you were gonna spend some time with her?"

"I was, but something came up."

He was on his way to meet one of his business associates. She understood. He then handed her an envelope filled with cash and left. As he drove across town, he thought about the gangsters who failed to claim Harlem as their own.

Me? I'll never make the mistakes those cats made, he said to himself, pulling up in front of the Hampton Coop Complex.

Kevin Murdock, also known as Trigga, was holding his own and doing quite well. He and Black conducted business daily. The two friends had attended middle and high school with Speedy, Riff, Justice, and Half Pint. Growing up in a Jamaican community in Harlem, their families were close. As youngsters, they partied hard, fought hard, and slept with the same girls. They supported each other and had a lasting friendship. Their motto was "family for life."

Brown skin with wavy hair, light brown eyes, and a slim physique, Trigga stood six feet. The leader of a Jamaican crew called the Jiggy Mob. His organization was a major player in the distribution and sales of drugs throughout the city. He conducted his business from West One Hundred and Twentieth Street to One Hundred and Twenty-Seventh Street and Manhattan Avenue. Feared for his pension to end an argument with a bullet and his sinister smile, Trigga was a force vying for control of the drug trade in Harlem.

"Waddup, Black?" Trigga asked with a slight Jamaican accent, checking out several packets of cocaine.

"I'm cool, son. Is this the new 'caine you were telling me about?"

"Yeah, this shit is pure. You can cut this as many times as you like," Trigga said, gesturing with his hand.

"You serious, son?"

"Yeah, I'm serious. Taste this."

Black dipped his finger in the cocaine and put it in his mouth.

"Damn! This Indo is strong."

"What did I tell you?" Trigga said laughing.

"We're gonna have to talk."

"No doubt! Yo, I heard that Half is still running off with the mouth."

"Yo, you know how that mutha-fucka is. Son, he was living foul rude boy. That's why I moved on his ass. I had to give him a reality check, you feel me?"

"That's real talk, son. So, you brought him back to reality?"

"No doubt, I had to do what I had to do."

"That's what's up. Yo, I have that thing for you."

"Cool. You have the whole thing?"

"Yeah, man, you done know."

"Hold this." He handed Trigga a brown paper bag filled with cash. Trigga then handed him the package.

"Yo, check this out and let me know what you think," Trigga said dipping his hand in a bag of Tai weed and giving him a handful.

"Cool, I'll get at you later," Black said.

EPISODE 5

Black was in an informative mood later that day, and as he began talking to several of his young workers about the drug trade, crack cocaine and its rapid ascent, and its devastating impact on urban America, he was pleased with his young audience's attentive behavior.

"A lot of cats thought this crack shit was over, but I'm here to tell y'all that shit never happened and will never happen. We getting rich off this bitch. We hustlers 'till we die. Y'all see those mutha-fuckas over there? Look at them! Crack did that!" Black said, pointing from the window at a group of crack heads standing on the corner.

"Damn, son, they look grimey," one of the kids said.

"Grimey ain't the mutha-fucking word. This bitch is dead. Mutha-fuckas were dying back in the day and are still dying. Niggas were sleeping. They ain't realize that this shit was gonna take off again. Those fat cats down at City Hall, and all these other mutha-fuckas y'all see running around here with legal guns and badges, they the ones bringing that shit in our hoods. Now y'all little mutha-fuckas wanna know why I said that shit, right? Come on ask, let me hear what y'all got to say," Black looked at them waiting for a response.

"Y'all little mutha-fuckas ain't got shit to say?" Speedy added smiling.

"I don't know what to say," a chubby kid said.

"Well, when these cats with the badges bring that shit in, we sell that shit to those mutha-fuckas you see over there, because we ain't like them. We are strong and they are fucking weak," Black stated, pointing at the same group of crack heads.

"Y'all don't wanna be on that list," Speedy warned them.

They had a pensive look on their faces as they stared at Black, Speedy, Riff, and then at themselves and the group of crack heads.

"See us, look at me," Black challenged them, pointing at himself. "We are filling their prescriptions. The shit needs to be filled, and it's our job to mend their broken hearts and minds. Harlem hospital can't help their sorry asses," Black exclaimed. They were laughing.

"Ain't that the same shit Frank Lucas, Nicky Barnes, and those cats used to do back in the day?" Riff asked.

"Yeah, they were doing shit like that, they got paid filling their prescriptions," Speedy added.

"They were selling heroin, cocaine, and running numbers. Mutha-fuckas were robbing and doing all sorts of wild shit to get a hit. But this crack shit? Those cats never had to deal with anything like this shit. This shit had mutha-fuckas killing each other. That's how it was in the 1980s and early '90s. Mutha-fuckas were trifling," Black went on.

The workers who weren't aware of the history of Frank Lucas and Nicky Barnes, and those who were mere babies when the crack epidemic was at its height, were awestruck. Their mouths were wide open as they listened to Black.

"Some of the older cats that me and Speedy wanted to run with when we were your ages, got snatched," he continued. "Niggas were merking their grandmothers, uncles, cousins, nieces and raping their sisters. Mutha-fuckas wasn't used to this type of shit. This was some different shit. Mutha-fuckas was off the chain. They were dumbing out. Y'all see those cats down on Wall Street, they wasn't into stocks and bonds anymore. Those mutha-fuckas were base heads."

"Word!" Riff added. "The hood was flooded with drugs. This crack shit was no joke."

The men told stories about lawyers, doctors, corporate CEOs, and cops who were addicted to the drug and blew their paychecks, law practices, and career for a night of unadulterated crack binges. Black warned them of the danger of its usage and how addictive, deadly and unapologetic the drug is.

"I bet some of y'all family members were hooked on that shit, weren't they?" Black asked. They were silent.

"Y'all ain't got to respond, we know the deal," Speedy said.

"Shit like that happens a lot, and I don't wanna hear any of you little mutha-fuckas getting hooked on that shit. Y'all feel me?" Black warned.

"We won't," they said.

"Next thing we know our papers are coming up short. We don't play that bullshit. We ain't with that down low incognito bullshit, y'all with me? We'll take you out in a minute, just like that, right, fellas?"

"No doubt, just like that," Speedy and Riff replied. Like clockwork, the young workers nodded in unison as they stared at each other as Black ended his impromptu conversation.

The community center where Black did most of his recruiting also profited from his philanthropist generosity. The young kids admired and looked up to him. Many of whom were from broken homes where there was a lack of parental control. Few, if any respected or looked up to any positive male figures. Therefore, it was easy for Black to make an impression on them. They had become accustomed to the few dollars he would personally hand out. Young and impressionable, they were fascinated by the thugs' life, the bling, and the whole gangster hype. They would do anything for him.

***

The summer had ended, and school was about to begin. Black felt good about the prospect and progress the crew had made, despite losing several of his young workers who returned to school. The ones who remained were quickly promoted. They were relocated to cities such as Hartford, Chapel Hills, Norfolk, and Denver, where his crew had set up their business. And as the year progressed, he began vast recruitment throughout the five boroughs of New York City.

Speedy was his right-hand man and minister of war. Suzy was in charge of recruitment and job promotions. Blaze was responsible for the direct operation of the drug houses. He was also an enforcer. Guys like Fats, Bee, Riff, and Crip were in charge of the foot soldiers. Justice who kept in contact with Black and had a job waiting for him once his stint in the army was over, was eagerly anticipating his discharge date upon hearing how well the organization was doing.

Blaze, Fats, and Bee were childhood friends of Joe. Joe, who was ten years older than Black, was a brother who never had any run-ins with the law until he got down on his luck. Blaze, Fats, and Bee were college graduates, whose lives had hit rock bottom.

Blaze lost his job as an accountant on Wall Street. He was involved in an embezzlement scandal where millions were stolen. Despite being a minor player, he was one of the first to be terminated and jailed. Fats, a former high school teacher, was fired for having an affair with one of his female students. Somehow, he managed to avoid jail time. Bee, an ex- police officer, was fired and prosecuted for accepting money from several of Brooklyn's most notorious drug dealers.

After getting fired from his job as an insurance agent, Joe and his ex-college buddies who were also doing badly rekindled their off-and-on business venture of "can't miss money scheme" on anyone they could sucker and con out of their money. Still down on their luck, they decided to get into the drug game. Things weren't looking good for Joe and his buddies until Black came to their rescue.

So, it wasn't a problem when Joe told them that Black was offering them a job. The thing that worried them most was taking orders from him. But after sitting down with Joe and talking it over, they put their egos aside and took him up on his offer.

Known as the Syndicate, Black's crew experienced its first serious altercation when members of the Webster Avenue crew hijacked one of their drug houses in Spanish Harlem. Ness, a young brother brought into the organization by Speedy, was in the house and barely made it out alive.

"Who the fuck these niggas think they are?" Black said to Speedy.

"I don't know, son. But we gotta put the heat on these mutha-fuckas," he replied.

"Tell Blaze to take care of that shit!" he ordered.

"I'm on it."

Several days later, two members of the Webster Avenue crew were shot to death as they entered an apartment building in the Wakefield section of the Bronx. The police wasted no time, as their informant provided the license plate numbers of the cars used in the killing. It didn't take long before three members of the Syndicate were arrested.

"You heard anything yet?" Black demanded.

"Yeah," Speedy informed him.

"And?"

"It's some dude name Skip from the Bronx. Dude is a straight-up crack head and snitch."

"I don't give a fuck! Do him!" Black commanded.

A week later Skip was gunned down and found hanged with his tongue missing in an abandoned building in the South Bronx. With their informant dead, the police had no choice but to release the three Syndicate members into the custody of their high-profile lawyers. Black was more than pleased when he received the news and immediately told Speedy to go and congratulate the men.

"See what I mean? That's how they protect their informants?" Black asked, waiting for an answer.

"Bitch ass snitches! I hate those mutha-fuckas!" Speedy snapped.

"It's like my homie, Trigga always say, '*Informa fi dead*!' straight," Black said aloud, as Speedy smiled. His smile was subtle. The Syndicate was expanding its control over the booming crack market while continuing its assault on anyone who dared to get in its way.

***

One week later . . .

Half Pint was hanging out with his cousin, Andre Campbell, also known as Homicide, and recently released from Attica state prison, after serving five years of a three-to-nine sentence for armed robbery. Their crew was hyped upon his release. Homicide had controlled the drug operations at the Polo Grounds before his incarceration. It was only after his imprisonment that Half Pint took control. Homicide's reputation was well known, and Half Pint saw to it that he was well taken care of.

Half Pint heard through the wire that Black and his crew were making a lot of money. And he hadn't forgotten the beating or his near-death experience at their hands. As he, Homicide, Lil Jay, and Trey headed downtown in a spanking baby blue Escalade, they decided to get something to eat. While Trey parked the ride, Half Pint couldn't believe his eyes. There in front of him stood Riff and his cousin, Daryl, who were oblivious to his presence. They were cornered as they waited in line at the Fish and Chip joint on the corner of St. Nicholas and One Hundred and Forty-Fifth Street. Daryl, who had bought his food minutes before Half Pint and his partners showed up, decided to wait for Riff, a huge mistake.

"Payback is a bitch, isn't it, Riff?" Half Pint said with a snarl as he reached in his waistband for his Glock.

"Yo, Daryl, get the fuck outta here!" Riff screamed to his cousin, reaching for his weapon. The sound of gunfire echoed across the avenue as people dove for cover.

Daryl reacted too late and several slugs from Homicide's weapon tore into his chest as the fish and chips flew harmlessly skyward. The smell of gun powder and fried fish filled the air as the rapid gun fire continued. Seeing his cousin hit, Riff began blasting away. Trey was hit three times in the head and hit the concrete, shaking. Half Pint returned fire along with Homicide and Lil Jay, but Riff wasn't backing down.

"Yo, let's get the fuck outta here!" Homicide yelled to Half Pint and Lil Jay.

"Nah. Let's do this punk. Fuck that!" Half Pint said angrily. Homicide was pissed.

"What the fuck is wrong with you? Let's bounce; I'm still on parole, son," he yelled at Half Pint.

If it weren't for the sirens from the approaching police cars, Half Pint would have kept on firing. Riff didn't have any second thoughts about getting into his car, knowing Daryl was dead. Half Pint, Homicide, and Lil Jay were heading to the Escalade when Homicide yelled, "Trey had the fucking keys."

"Fuck!" Half Pint yelled. "Jay, go get the keys."

While Lil Jay ran over to Trey's body, Homicide shouted, "I'm out!"

He bolted up One Hundred and Forty-Fifth Street, turned right on Convent Avenue, and took off like he was running the hundred-meter dash. Lil Jay found the keys. He and Half Pint got in the Escalade and hauled ass seconds before the first patrol cars pulled up.

When Riff got back to the safe house, he was having some difficulty breathing, and as he began explaining what happened, Black told him to relax and to take his time. The trauma on his face was conspicuous as he began recounting what happened.

"I didn't see those bitches! Fuck!" he rambled on, trying to compose himself.

"Those mutha-fuckas are going down; believe that," Black said in a cold emotionless voice.

"But . . ."

"Don't sweat it. You'll get yours," Black said confidently.

"I know, but damn!" he kept repeating.

"So that pussy Homicide was there too, huh?" Black said out loud.

"Yeah. I didn't know that bitch ass mutha-fucka was out. He's the one who took Daryl out," he said angrily, as Black tried to calm him down. Black didn't say another word. He put his arm around him and nodded his head as an older brother would.

EPISODE 6

Following Daryl's death, The Get Paid crew began sending death threats to the Syndicate. This forced Speedy to be more cautious as he made his nightly rendezvous to One Hundred and Fifty-Third Street and Lenox Avenue, where his new girlfriend Peaches lived. Speedy was convinced that Half Pint and his crew were becoming a thorn in the side of the Syndicate and had to be dealt with sooner rather than later. And he was prepared to take matters into his hand.

Peaches was sitting on the stoop with her friends late one night when a silver Mercedes Benz came to a screeching halt in front of the building where they sat. Inside the car were Half Pint and Lil Jay. Peaches, aware of the bad blood between Speedy and Half Pint, quickly recognized him. As Half Pint exited the car, he smiled at the girls and glanced up and down the block before entering the lobby of the building.

"That's a fly ass ride, and whose man is that?" Peaches asked wanting to know if any of her friends were dating him.

"That's that stuck-up bitch, Ashley's man," her friend Tata said in a jealous tone.

"Is that the girl who drives the white Pathfinder?" Peaches asked.

"Yeah, that's her," Tata continued.

"That's the bitch you always hate on, right, Tata?" Peaches said, laughing.

"I don't hate on her. I don't know why y'all listening to this bitch," Tata laughed aloud.

"Let me move to the side 'cause this bitch is lying. And I don't wanna get hit by lightning tonight. Y'all better move," Peaches continued laughing with her girls.

"Oh, well, she isn't all that," Tata remarked rolling her eyes as Peaches agreed with her.

Although Peaches cared for Speedy, she was somewhat hesitant and fearful about telling him that Half Pint was seeing Ashley. Ashley, a fine-looking red bone, had been dating Half Pint, off and on for a year. She had recently moved out of the Polo Grounds and into her apartment. Half Pint knew that his enemies frequented the neighborhood and like Speedy, he took precautionary measures and visited late at night.

One night after dinner and a movie, Speedy's suspicions were aroused. For the past two weeks, Peaches had asked him to drop her at her grandmother's apartment instead of her own. When he questioned her about it, she said her grandmother was ill. What he didn't know was that she would walk home from there. Not one to argue, he left it alone. Her reasons for saying and doing those things were that she didn't want to get involved in his affairs. But as faith would have it, she, Speedy, and Half Pint would cross paths.

The following weekend after partying at Club Hurricane, Speedy and Peaches rolled up on the corner of One Hundred and Fifty-Third Street and Lenox Avenue. As they waited for the light to make the right turn onto One Hundred and Fifty-Third Street, Peaches' worst nightmares were about to come true, when she suddenly yelled, "There goes Half!"

Initially, she didn't want to say anything, but she wasn't sure if Speedy saw him. Nonetheless, she got an immediate response.

"Where?" Speedy yelled, his eyes darting back and forth along the avenue paying particular attention to a group of men, who were talking and drinking amongst themselves. She was upset at herself because she had spoken too soon, but by then it was too late. It was obvious that Speedy never saw him.

"Right there in that car," she said, pointing in the direction of Wendy's restaurant on the corner.

"Which car?" he asked, his weapon now drawn.

"The silver Benz."

"Are you sure that's his car?" His eyes were filled with hate.

"Yeah, that's his car."

Speedy wasn't familiar with the silver Benz with its engine running in the parking lot of the Wendy's Restaurant. He wanted to make sure it was Half Pint behind the wheel. He kissed Peaches good night and said, "Make sure it's him, a'ight. Take a quick peek, and if it's him call me."

"A'ight," she replied, nodding her head. He didn't want any mishaps, as he kept his eyes on the Benz.

Inside the car were Half Pint and one of his underlings. Despite how she felt about Ashley, she was relieved knowing that she wasn't in the car as she pulled out her cell phone.

"It's him!" Peaches said.

"A'ight, are you in the building?" he asked, coolly.

"No, almost."

"Are you there now?"

"Yeah, I'm waiting for the elevator."

"Later," he said.

Alighting from his car, gun in hand; Speedy cautiously crept up to the driver's side of the Benz without either man seeing him, and let loose a barrage of bullets. Peaches cringed when she heard the gun shots. She looked out her window. The shots echoed into the quiet night as Half Pint somehow managed to get the car started. It veered and swerved out of control before crashing into the concrete embankment in the middle of Lenox Avenue. Speedy figured they were dead. But he didn't want any mistakes. Mistakes weren't an option. He emptied his clip in the silver Benz.

As the gun shots peppered the street, several sleepless New Yorkers ran for cover in the buildings and others hid behind parked cars. Positive that no one could have survived the rain of bullets that he fired into the car, Speedy took several glances, making sure he wasn't seen; he then rushed to his car and drove off. Several of the spectators gradually made their way over to the bodies. Inside the car, the bodies of the blood-splattered men were slumped over in their seats. Half Pint's partner was barely breathing, but the same couldn't be said for him. His shocked face was still like the night. There wasn't a pinch of life in him. His partner later died on the way to the hospital.

Upon hearing the news, Black snapped, "Fuck that, nigga! He had that shit coming. I should have merked his ass that night in the Polo Grounds."

"Word! Fuck that! Bitch ass mutha-fucka!" Riff concurred, feeling some closure.

"Just be careful, a'ight? You know they're gonna come at us, so watch your backs and don't sleep."

"We know," the others stated.

"Any messages for me, Speedy?" Black asked.

"Yeah. Trigga stopped by earlier."

"Oh, yeah! That means he's got the work. Come on, ride with me."

"A'ight, I'm with it."

They headed down the stairs and got in the car, when Black said, "Yo, Maria is pregnant."

"Word?"

"Yeah, son, she told me earlier."

"Son, that's cool! Uncle Speedy, I like it." They laughed as Black drove off.

"Yeah, son, that's what it's all about; family, you feel me?"

"No doubt, Black! I'm happy for you and Maria, word."

"Thanks, bro, that's what's up!" Black said as they pulled up on Trigga's block.

EPISODE 7

Two weeks later…

There was some in-fighting going on between the upper echelon members of the Get Paid Crew and Homicide for control of the organization, after Half Pint's death. Although he faced some resistance, Homicide eventually won them over and took over the leadership. He immediately vowed revenge.

"That bitch ass mutha-fucka Black and his dawgs are gonna feel my heat," Homicide bragged to Lil Jay as he drove up One Hundred and Twenty-Fifth Street towards the Henry Hudson Parkway. After taking care of their business, the men drove to Nu- Cars Limited on Fordham Road, in the Bronx, where Lil Jay's ride was getting detailed.

"Yo, why don't you wait for me, and we can ride back together," Lil Jay suggested to Homicide.

"Son, your shit ain't even ready, plus I gotta pick up this little shorty from Grant projects. This bitch ain't used to shit so Im'a take her to the

Hotel Plaza Athenee and let her have some fun for two nights, you know what am saying?"

"No doubt, a'ight," Lil Jay said, smiling. "Be safe, yo."

"Get at me if you need me, a'ight."

"Cool."

"A'ight," Homicide said, as he sped off.

Within minutes, he was at the Grant Houses where he picked up his date and drove to the Hotel Plaza Athenee on East Sixty-Fourth Street on the upper eastside of Manhattan. He never saw the black C L 330 Mercedes Benz that followed him.

***

Through their informants, the Syndicate got word that Homicide would be staying a second night. That night, two male figures dressed in black pants and white shirts entered the lobby of the Hotel. The men had a nervous look on their faces as they reassured each other that things would go well. As they observed the other workers in the lobby, their confidence grew as the uniforms they wore blended in nicely with the other workers. The lobby was filled with people checking in and out.

The men walked past the busy front desk, making eye contact with the two young women, who were busy taking care of the guests; there was no reaction from the women as they walked toward the elevator.

"Are you sure it's room six-twenty-four?" Riff asked as he and Speedy were greeted by the voice of Tom Jones singing, "It's Not Unusual."

"No doubt," Speedy stated, as the elevator came to a stop on the sixth floor.

"Thank, God!" Riff exhaled.

"What's that for?"

"That whack-ass music was killing me."

"Damn, son!" Speedy said. "You only rode the mutha-fucka six flights up."

"I know, but I couldn't stand seeing Carlton Banks from the "Fresh Prince of Bel-Air," singing and dancing to that shit," he said as both men smiled.

Straightening out their uniforms they looked at each other and said, "Let's do this!"

There was a serious look on their faces as they exited the elevator and headed down the hallway. Their eyes were fixed on the numbers of each room they passed.

"Here it is," Riff said.

"Remember, stick to the plan."

"Cool," Riff replied, nodding in agreement as his eyes darted up and down the hallway.

"Hello." It was a precocious little girl who was walking to the elevator with her family.

"Oh, hi!" both men replied, obviously surprised as the family got on the elevator. Speedy knocked on the door.

"Who is it?" an agitated female voice asked. It was obvious she didn't want to be bothered.

"Room service."

"Give me a minute." The door opened, and a sexy young girl with a sheet draped over her body asked, "What is . . .?"

Startled, and taken aback by the presence of the two men, she never got to finish her sentence. Speedy quickly stuck his gun with its silencer attached to her face, placed his finger over his lips, and said, "Shh." The sound of running water was coming from the bathroom. On the bed were a chrome-plated nine-millimeter Glock, a gun holster, and a du-rag. The element of surprise was working in their favor, as Riff quickly pulled a pair of handcuffs from his back pocket, cuffed the young lady to the bed post, and duct-taped her mouth, while Speedy quietly entered the bathroom.

"Get the fuck out the shower, mutha-fucka!" Speedy yelled as he viciously busted Homicide over the head with the handle of his gun.

"What the fuck is this?" a visibly shaken Homicide pleaded his eyes filled with fear.

"Get the fuck over there!" Speedy snapped shoving him as he cowered into the bedroom.

"Your worst nightmare, mutha-fucka!" Riff said bashing him in the mouth.

A feeling of anxiety, fright, horror, and terror overcame Homicide, as he pleaded, "It's not like that, yo! What y'all want money, cars, a piece of the action, what?"

"Did you hear what this mutha-fucka just said? Did he ask if we wanted money and cars?" Riff snapped.

"It ain't got to go down like this!" Homicide cried getting on his knees.

"Shut the fuck up, bitch! This shit is a rap!" Speedy said as he handcuffed and gagged him.

"Is he your man?" Riff asked the young girl. She shook her head, no. He walked over to her and removed the duct tape from her mouth.

"Please!" she begged, as the realization of death dawned on her. She had a terrified look on her face as she stared at Speedy and Riff.

"I'll be quiet. I don't wanna die! I'll suck your dick! You wanna fuck me? You can fuck me! I'll do anything for you! Just don't kill me!" she sobbed wide-eyed blinking frantically.

Homicide's face was the epitome of horror as he grimaced, knowing that his fate was sealed. His words were muffled as Speedy smothered his face with one of the pillows. Riff calmly approached him and pulled the trigger. Two rounds slammed into the head of Homicide, killing him instantly. The young girl was hysterical. She was going out of her mind. Her eyes were rolling back and forth. She lifted her body off the bed, thrashing from side to side. Saliva was foaming from the corners of her mouth.

"Let her go," Riff said, seeing the look of pity and desperation in her eyes.

"No doubt," Speedy replied as he smiled, smacked his lips, turned, and fired a bullet into her forehead. Her body began convulsing as blood poured from the wound.

"Waddup with that, Speedy?" Riff asked visibly upset.

"No witnesses, Black's orders," he said with a sinister smile. "You do a job; you do it the right way. That cute face and pussy got you hot, huh?"

"Nah. Son, she was only a fuck. She had nothin' to do with that mutha-fucka!"

"You right, but like Black says, no witnesses," he repeated as they scrambled down the stairs. They were huffing and puffing as they hit the lobby. Everything was normal, there wasn't any suspicious or unusual activity going on as they composed themselves and walked out the door.

***

Not long after Speedy and Peaches ended their relationship, she began dating a brother named Low. From the St. Nicholas housing project in Harlem, Low had an ongoing business relationship with the Get Paid crew, which Peaches wasn't aware of. They were hanging out one night when he decided to stop at the Wagner houses.

"Are you coming? Or you wanna wait?" Low asked her.

"I ain't staying out here by myself with all these wild ass niggas."

"Well, come on then." There was a group of young men hanging out in the lobby of the building when Low and Peaches entered.

"What's poppin, Low?" one of the men said his eyes glued to the dice game he was playing with several of his cronies.

"I'm cool. Is Big L upstairs?"

"Yeah, he up there."

"A'ight, later y'all."

Peaches had an uneasy look on her face as she entered the apartment. Inside were Big L, Killa Mike, and Sasha, they were busy cooking up several kilos of cocaine into crack.

"What's poppin', son? What's good?" Big L asked.

"I came to get that," Low responded, greeting the others.

"You got all the money?"

"Yeah, son, but why you be asking shit like that?"

"Come on, son. Don't get shit twisted. The last time I had to wait an extra two hours for the rest of my money."

"Well, you ain't got to wait this time. I got it."

"Yo, Sasha, go in the room and get me the package on the dresser."

After handing the package to Big L, Sasha called Killa Mike to the side, "Yo, that bitch with Low, she looks familiar."

"Word?"

"Yeah. I think that's the bitch that set up Half."

"What! Are you sure? Yo, don't be saying shit that you know ain't right."

"Yeah, I'm sure that's the bitch, and I ain't making shit up. Let me holla at Tiny, she'll know."

Killa Mike immediately told Big L what was going on. Low was getting ready to leave when Big L stuck his Uzi in his face.

"Just chill, son! Keep your fucking hands where I can see them. Mike, get his gun," Big L snarled.

Astonished, Low was rendered speechless as his life flashed in front of his eyes. With Low now disarmed, Big L snatched Peaches up and began slapping her around.

"Yo, L, what the fuck did she do? What the fuck is up?" Low asked in a shaken and concerned voice. Big L was about to respond when there was a knock on the door and in walked Tiny as Peaches began screaming and yelling.

"Shut the fuck up, bitch! Get your ass over there!" Killa Mike barked at her.

"Is this the bitch, Tiny?" Big L snapped.

"Yeah, that's her, L."

"I told you!" Sasha said, glancing over at Peaches.

"What the fuck she did?" Low pleaded, about to get the shock of his life.

"This bitch set up Half!" a pissed Big L stated with a screw face.

"What? Did she set up Half? Oh, shit! I was fucking with this bitch, and she played out my dawg?" a furious Low hollered.

"Yo, we ain't know what was up with you and this bitch!" Big L said.

"This bitch told me her name was Tricia," Low said angrily. "I can't believe this shit!"

"Tricia? The bitch name is Peaches, and this shit is a rap. A brotha had to make sure, that's all, no hard feelings, a'ight, here's your burner," Big L said handing Low his Glock.

"Please, Low! It wasn't me! It wasn't me!" Peaches screamed.

"Who is it then?" he asked. "Just tell them who it is."

"I don't know, but it wasn't me!"

"You keep saying it ain't you, so who is it then?"

"I, don't know," she sobbed. Low was dumbfounded as he shakes his head in disbelief.

Tiny would have none of the sobbing, theatrics, or denials as she snapped at Peaches, "It was you bitch, Ashley, and them knew it was you. You was fucking with that dude Speedy, don't lie, bitch! Even those bitches you hung out with said, you always hated on Ashley."

"No, no, it wasn't me! Please, let me go! Low, don't leave me here! I'm begging you!"

Bristling under his breath, Low and the men exchanged fist bumps and walked out the door. Pleading and begging for her life, Killa Mike took her into the bedroom and turned the volume up on the CD player. He told her to sit on the bed, which she did.

"I swear! I didn't set him up. Me and Speedy went to the movies and then he drove me home. After I got in my building, I heard shots."

"And you ain't think it was your man?" Killa Mike asked.

"Yeah. I called him, but he said it wasn't him; it was some dudes on the block. So, I left it alone. I swear!"

"And that's the truth?"

"Yeah. Can I please go home now? Can I?"

"Yeah, you going home don't worry about it,"

Killa Mike snarled while attaching the silencer to his weapon.

He shoved the gun in her face as she began to wail. His response was a bullet to her head as she fell on her back, dead.

"Sasha, get the bags and make sure you clean the place up," Big L commanded. Later that night, Peaches' body was dumped in Hunts Point.

EPISODE 8

Life had changed dramatically for Mrs. Reynolds. She was under constant pressure from Black to quit her job. And when she did, she did so, with some apprehension. Black immediately put her in charge of the newly owned laundromat businesses he started. The businesses, along with several others were family-operated. Several of Mrs. Reynold's close friends were hired as workers. Black was relieved to see his mother and family members not having to work as hard as they did in the past. This meant a lot to him, as he reminisced on the many lonely nights, he and Adiba would be home alone, while their mother worked the graveyard shift. *Yeah, I like this much better,* he said to himself, smiling.

Mrs. Reynolds would get the shock of her life several months later, when he drove her and Adiba to the suburbs of Massapequa, Long Island, and showed them the home he bought for them. She was ecstatic, as he drove up to the house and saw how beautiful it was. Black was happy for her. She was beaming with delight as she thanked him.

"It's nothin' ma, you deserve this," he said. She hugged him, crying.

"Thank you, son," she replied as she and Adiba checked out the swimming pool.

"Ma, are you gonna come swimming with me?" Adiba asked, smiling.

"Child, you know I can't swim, that's for you young folks. I'll stay on dry land where I'm much safer," she said chuckling.

"I'm glad you did this for her. She deserves it," Adiba told him.

"Yeah, baby sis, I'm glad for her too, but it's for you too now."

"I know, but look at her, she can't stop crying."

I love you, Dante," Adiba said, hugging him.

Black certainly didn't stop there; he was living lovely and relishing every moment of it. Soon thereafter, he purchased a stately mansion in the upscale neighborhood of Shorts Hills in Millburn Township, New Jersey. The house was built with the latest design and technology. Inside the rooms were state-of-the-art cameras and monitors, which were linked to a private security company. On the premises were several huge trees and a heart-shaped pool. The lawn was beautifully manicured. The mansion was gated to keep out the unwanted and a guard house with twenty-four-hour security.

***

Two months later . . .

Black and Maria were elated as they awaited the arrival of their first child. Maria was familiar with Yvette and Jasmine. But what she wouldn't accept and tolerate were the other women and Black's womanizing ways. Nevertheless, she didn't let any of it prevent her from falling in love with him. So, when he proposed to her, she did not hesitate in saying, yes. She was happy as they settled into married life with their new baby girl, Chyan. They were having the time of their lives. They had lots of family and friends and they partied a lot. The parties at their mansion were wild. There was always a steady stream of weed and alcohol. Their family and friends would end up spending the night after hours of unadulterated partying. Black never had a problem with any of it. He knew that Maria enjoyed it, and he wanted to make her happy.

***

But as luck would have it, the few days of sharing and relaxing with family and friends would end with his arrest, as he unknowingly drove into a checkpoint the police had set up on Lenox Avenue and One Hundred and Forty-Seventh Street. He was pulled over and searched. A hand gun was found under his seat. He was immediately arrested and taken to Central Booking. He was pissed, as the hours passed without a phone call. To make matters worse, there were several men in the bullpen next to him making all sorts of threats.

"I hope you make this bus to the island!" one of them hollered.

"Fuck, you! You bitch ass mutha-fucka!" Black snarled in a challenging voice.

"This nigga got a lot of bass in his voice," the man added as the others laughed.

"Tell y'all what? When we get to the island, we'll deal with this shit!"

"Fuck you, Black! Punk ass mutha-fucka!" he continued.

"You'll see how much of a punk I am! You bitch ass!"

"Shut the fuck up! Be quiet ladies, save that nonsense for the island!" a burly Newport smoking correction officer yelled.

"Fuck you, CO! Where's my phone call?" Black asked fearlessly.

"You better watch your mouth mutha-fucka! If I, were you, I would be quiet so I can get my phone call," he said showing considerable restraint.

A comment like that would have led to an ass-kicking, but the officer's shift was almost over. Black certainly didn't want to make the trip to Rikers Island. He knew he would have to crack a few heads if he was put on the bus.

"Reynolds! You're next!" the correction officer barked.

It's about time, Black said to himself, relating what had transpired to Speedy, as they talked on the phone. He was more than happy to make night court, where his bail was set at thirty-five hundred dollars, which was immediately posted.

***

The next day, Black visited Trigga.

"My youth, you a crazy mutha-fucka!" Trigga exclaimed.

"What's up? What the fuck you talking about?" Black smiled.

"Half Pint and Homicide homies are tight. They shot up Moments nightclub, thinking y'all was up in there."

"Fuck them mutha-fuckas, son! They took out Riff, cuz. You know we ain't going out like that."

"True that! They had that shit coming. They been fighting us for a long time, yo."

"Well, they ain't fighting no more."

"For real. Fuck them niggas! Yo, here's the thing I promised you. I know you living large." He laughed.

"We eating lovely," Black said as they laughed.

"Remember them fools I was telling you about?"

"Yeah, waddup with them fools from Washington Heights?"

"Me and my dawgs gave them a check a few nights ago."

"That was y'all?"

"Yeah, man."

"I heard like two mutha-fuckas got clapped up."

"You done know rude boy, we had to keep it real; and any pussy test, we taking them out."

"That's right, son. By the way, my mom says, hi."

"Tell Mrs. Reynolds I say, hi. How is she?"

"She is still the same. She still wilding, but she toned it down though."

"Yeah, right," Trigga said as they fell out laughing, remembering how strict she was.

"So how is your mom?"

"She cool rude boy."

"Tell her I said, hi."

"Yeah, man. Yo, when last you chat to Divine?"

"It's been a minute to tell you the truth, word; I gotta hit him up."

"For real."

"That mutha-fucka is stacking, he done forget about us," Black laughed.

"No wonder he's keeping a low profile."

"If you hit that mutha-fucka up before me, tell him to give me a check. I gotta make a run. I'll get back to you."

"A'ight, be safe my nig."

"No doubt!" Black replied.

EPISODE 9

One month later . . .

Several members of the Syndicate were chilling at the main stash house when Suzy informed them of Crip's death. Upon hearing the news, Fats told him to contact Black, and he would notify Speedy.

"What the fuck happened?" Black asked with a puzzled look on his face.

"The Webster Avenue crew merked him!" Suzy said out of breath.

"Where's Speedy and them?"

"They on their way."

"A'ight, I'll be there in a few."

Only nineteen years old, Black had taken a likening to Crip. He took him under his wing, taking him along on many of his business rendezvous. But over the last month and a half, Suzy put him in charge of several drug houses in the Crotona Park section of the Bronx.

Despite the constant threats from the Webster Avenue crew, who also did business in the same neighborhood, the Syndicate was making a lot of money and had no intention of giving up their drug houses. Initially, Black was against Crip's promotion, fearing it was too dangerous for someone as young as him. But after talking it over with him, he somehow convinced Black that he could handle it.

It was a relatively easy job. He always had his weapon. He was careful whenever he made his rounds. He lived at Ninety-Sixth Street and Central Park West, with his girlfriend and young daughter. He drove a 2003 Lexus SUV. Black never had a problem with him. He lived up to his end of the deal. But things were about to unravel on this particular night, as he made a left turn from Boston Road onto Crotona Park.

Pulling up across the street from one of the Syndicate drug houses, he peeped out his surroundings and alighted from his car. In his hand was a package containing five hundred capsules of crack cocaine. He entered the building, taking the stairs to the second-floor apartment. Once inside, he hands the package to one of the workers, who handed over the day's profit.

"I'll see y'all later," he said walking out the door. Hitting the street, he followed his normal routine. Seeing that everything was fine, he walked toward his ride. He was about to get in when a young girl suddenly appeared out of nowhere and said, hi.

Damn! She looks good! He thought. He wasted no time in striking up a conversation. They were about to exchange numbers when three men suddenly burst around the corner with their guns blazing and blasting away at him. He dove for cover inside his Lexus as they rushed him and pumped several rounds into his body. He tried valiantly to return their fire, but it was too late.

He turned around in time to see the young girl aiming a .357 magnum at his head. She pumped two rounds in the back of his head.

His body slumped onto the black leather of the passenger side seat of the Lexus, his lifeless body lying like a rag doll. She picked up the bag from the seat of the car and ran to a waiting black Yukon, which sped off.

"Listen! Did you tell his parents?" Black asked Suzy wanting to know if Speedy had arrived.

"Nah, not yet."

"Good. I'm almost there."

"A'ight."

When he arrived at the safe house, Black told Speedy to contact Crip's mother and his girlfriend and to let them know that he'll take care of the funeral arraignments. He gave fifty-thousand dollars to his girlfriend and daughter and told her if she needed anything in the future, to give him a call.

***

Some time had passed when Black sat down with several key members of the crew. He informed them that something had to be done about Crip's death. He felt the Webster Avenue crew had gone too far and they needed a wake-up call. After being assured that everyone understood their particular roles, he headed for the George Washington Bridge. As he drove home, he wondered who the young girl was and if Crip had any contact with her before his death. He had a lot of questions and he feared some of them would remain unanswered. But he knew he could find solace in Maria's arm. She was his most trusted confidante and despite the other women in his life, whenever he had a problem or needed a different perspective, he would turn to her.

"Crip was killed earlier tonight," he said to Maria entering the living room.

"Oh, my God! He was so young. Who did it?"

"The Webster Avenue crew."

"That is so sad. I feel bad for his girlfriend and daughter."

"Yeah, we contacted her and his mother and took care of the funeral arrangements."

"Already?"

"Yeah. Why?"

"Nothing, it's just that it was quick."

"Yeah. I know. But I knew she needed the help and the sooner the better."

Nodding in agreement, Maria said, "You're right."

"But now, I've got this shit over my head."

"What shit?"

"The gun charge. I can't afford to get locked down. I'm not with that." Maria listened intently to him and told him how she felt about losing him to jail or an early grave.

"Don't worry. My lawyers are taking care of things. I ain't going nowhere," he assured her despite the worried look.

"I hope so because I don't know what I would do."

Maria had been trying for some time to get him to give up the drug game. She was concerned about his safety, but she knew he wouldn't just give in and walk away. He hinted to her on several occasions that if he were to walk away from the game, what he would do. She reminded him that he owned several legitimate businesses. Hence, he could make the transition with the help of his high-powered lawyers.

“Honey, listen to me for a second. I can’t just get up and walk away from the business, leaving Speedy and Suzy in charge. I mean Speedy is cool and he understands the whole operation. I could see him running things, but Suzy? Come on, mama. He would wreck the business in a matter of months.” They both laughed at the thought of him running the operations. “Sure, my lawyers can help me with the legitimate business operations, but it’s gonna take a while.”

“But you have to start somewhere, Dante. Do you have a timetable?”

“No. I don’t, but . . .”

“All I’m saying is that you need to start looking into it.”

“Okay, I will.”

“You promise?”

“Yes. But on a serious note, mama, this is our life; it’s your life too. We in this together! Me and you.”

“Baby, I understand, that’s why I want you to think about going legit.”

“I promise I’ll think about it.”

“Okay, but can you do me a favor?”

“What’s that?”

“Can you come straight home once you’re done with your business? Or at least give me a call?”

“Sure, mama, that’s no problem.”

“I love you, Dante; you’re the best thing that ever happened to me.”

“The same goes for me, sweetheart.”

“I’m glad you feel the same way.”

“I do. And since you say you love me so much, why don’t you show me?” he smiled.

"I will!" Maria said giggling, pulling him into the bedroom.

EPISODE 10

Early the next morning, Black was aroused from his sleep by the ringing of his cell phone. It was Speedy. He wanted him to get to Harlem as soon as possible. Black knew something was wrong from the tone of his voice. He thought about asking him for more information but thought better of it as he hung up the phone. As he got himself together and said goodbye to his family, several scenarios began running through his mind.

Minutes later, he pulled up on the block. He parked and emerged, taking several long strides as he entered the vestibule of the building with its dimly lit lights. He entered the apartment where he was greeted by the rank and file of the organization.

"We got the niggas that killed Crip," Speedy uttered as the others looked on.

"Oh, yeah, where they at?" Black asked with an uneasy look on his face.

"At the house in the Bronx."

"By the way, how many of them?" he didn't wait for an answer as he said, "Let's roll!"

They headed down the stairs, moving rather quickly as they got into their rides.

"Where did you snatch these niggas at?" Black asked.

"Over by Reggie and them, we saw them leaving the building."

"And who are we?"

"Oh! It was me and Suzy," Speedy stated.

"Cool."

There was a loud bang on the door, Peanut and Jazz were inside the apartment and started shitting on themselves, believing it was the police.

"Open the fucking door!" Suzy yelled.

"Oh, a'ight, hold up," Peanut called out.

Black walked in without saying a word. He headed to the back of the apartment. There tied up and gagged were two scared-looking men. He removed the tape from their mouths and asked, "Who the fuck y'all worked for?"

"Worked for?" one of the men asked, realizing the impact and severity of his words. "Yo, man. It ain't got to be like this. I'm begging you!"

"Shut the fuck up and answer the question!" Black snapped with a menacing look on his face.

"The Webster Avenue crew!" both men blurted out.

The men swallowed hard and looked at each other. They wanted to know if they were going to go free. Black told them to trust their instinct. He was subjecting both men to mental anguish and verbal torment.

"Yo, Black, we only workers. All we do is deliver the shit and pick the shit up. We ain't got nothin' to do with the killings, Black, that's my word!"

"Y'all expect me to believe that shit, after what y'all did to my dawg? And how the fuck y'all know my name is, Black?"

"Your man told us only Black can save us. So, we figured you must be him," he stammered.

Eh, Black said to himself with a chuckle.

"Fuck this shit, Black! Let's do 'em!" Speedy snapped. Black smiled and then turned his attention back toward the men.

"What's your boss's name?"

"Big Jeff."

They were shocked to hear that Big Jeff was their boss. They were familiar with the name. Yet they were under the impression that someone else was in charge.

"You mean that big light skin mutha-fucka from Tremont and Jerome Avenue?" Black asked.

"Yeah, that's him," Speedy said.

"Is he still doing business up there?" Black asked waiting for the men to respond.

"Nah. But he got most of downtown Bronx and Crotona on lock," the other man said.

"What about Harlem?"

"He's got a few spots over there too," both men stuttered, crying.

"Here in Harlem?" Black snarled, nodding his head as he stared at them. Before they could respond, he looked the men in the eyes and said, "He's in my town? Where the fuck is he at?"

"He's at One Hundred and Fifty-Fifth Street and Amsterdam," the more talkative of the two men cried, as tears and snot began dripping on the floor.

"Son, these mutha-fuckas are crying like little bitches," Speedy snapped.

"Give me your burner Speedy," Black said with a snicker.

Without saying a word, Speedy handed him his .357 magnum. Black unloaded the gun except for one bullet. Putting the nozzle of the gun against the head of the man closest to him, he pulled the trigger, and nothing happened. He pissed all over himself as Black side-stepped the puddle on the floor. Smiling, he put the gun to the head of the other man and pulled the trigger. Boom! Blood and flesh splattered on the face of the other man and against the wall, and on Black. As his body slumped over, Black calmly handed the gun to Speedy.

"Yo, get rid of the body and do that other mutha-fucka," he said coldly, as Peanut handed him a wet rag.

"No doubt," Speedy responded. Knowing he was next; the man began hollering and crying.

"Fuck you, Black! Fuck that! I ain't going out like that! Yeah, we did that nigga! Mutha-fuckas suck my dick! Fuck, y'all!"

They were astounded as they stared at him. Speedy quickly shoved his .357 magnum in his mouth and pulled the trigger. The impact blasted a hole the size of a ping pong ball on the back of his neck. Blood and flesh were all over the place; it was a gory site as Speedy with a wild look in his eyes snickered and said, "Did you see that shit? I know y'all seen it! I blew his ass away!" Later that night, two bodies were found dumped off I-95.

"Speedy, how the fuck y'all didn't know about this?" Black wanted to know.

"What?"

"That this mutha-fucka, Big Jeff, was in Harlem in our backyard taking food out of our mouths and none of you knew about it? What the fuck is going on here? Y'all are slipping, or what?"

"I guess I'ma have to stay on their asses twenty-four seven. But that shit won't happen again. I'll make sure of that."

"You do that, Speedy. You make sure of that."

Black wasn't taking things lightly; he called his contacts and they responded immediately. They informed him that Big Jeff was in the neighborhood and that he should be careful because his connections were legitimate, and he was friends with several high-ranking police officials. Black was grateful for the information as he contemplated his next move.

***

After discussing it with his partners, Black and the crew agreed that their police contacts had to do something about Big Jeff. They wanted him dead. But their contacts were more interested in locking him up.

"Fuck that! We want that nigga dead!" Speedy exclaimed.

The other members of the crew were also opposed to the idea of Big Jeff rotting away in jail. As far as they were concerned, jail was the easy way out. They felt Big Jeff and his crew should pay for killing Crip. William Woods also known as Woody Woods was one of three corrupt cops in attendance at the meeting. He was an arrogant, mean-spirited bastard of a sergeant. His thing was to shake down the local dealers and confiscate their drugs, and then have them sell them to pay him off. Anyone who resisted ended up dead or in jail. He fabricated a lot of stories and got away with them. He created a long list of enemies. Taking the floor, he began telling the men how he was being pressured by his supervisors. But, if given the right amount of money, he could work something out.

"Gentlemen, you are talking about a serious matter here. With the money we are being offered right now, jail is a more viable option . . .," Woody didn't get to finish what he was saying.

"So, what are you trying to say?" Speedy interrupted.

"Hold on now. Let him finish," Black retorted.

"But Black, he wants more money for taking these niggas out, fuck that! They already getting sixty-thousand dollars. How much more do they want?" Speedy asked his voice rising.

"Okay, Woody, I'll give you guys a hundred grand that's it." Black stared at him with weary eyes.

"This is a large sum of money we're talking about here, Black. And if we take this money, I guess I would have to guarantee there won't be any problems, huh?"

"What the fuck do you think?" he responded with a blank stare.

"Well, I'll make sure of that."

"What the fuck you mean, 'I'll make sure of that?' This isn't about mistakes, Woody. If y'all can't handle it, let a mutha-fucka know right now. You getting paid a lot of money. So, there shouldn't be any problems, a'ight!" Speedy said angrily getting up from his seat.

Visibly upset and tired of hearing Speedy's mouth, Woody turned to Black and said, "Gentlemen, it's a deal, okay. Black, we will get the rest of the money once the problem has disappeared." They shook hands and closed the meeting.

***

Black was still talking with the others when his cell phone rang, it was his Aunt Shelly.

"Dante, there was a fire at the Laundromat," Shelly said shaken.

"Which one and is ma okay?" he asked nervously.

"The one on Lexington and yes, she's fine. Hurry and get over here."

Thank God! He said to himself, as the look of panic disappeared from his face. He bolted to his car along with Speedy. Within minutes, he was on the scene and as he pulled upon the block, he saw his mother and aunt hugging each other and crying. He walked over to them and reassured them he would find out who started the fire.

"No doubt!" Speedy yelled.

"Son, the fire chief believes it was an accident. They told me they would have more information for me tomorrow." They remained at the scene until the firemen told them they were no longer needed.

"Ma, they got all the information, let's go. It makes no sense being here right now."

"Okay, but what about my car? I can't leave it here."

"Aunty, can you drive it for me?"

"Sure, don't worry," she said, taking the keys.

"Im'a drop Spee . . . I mean Cory home, meet me over at Adiba."

"Okay."

After dropping Speedy at his apartment, Black drove to Riverside Drive with his mother to the apartment he recently bought for his sister. His mother, who had a key to the apartment, was too distraught to go to Long Island. Once inside the apartment, he called Maria and told her about the fire at the laundromat. Though exhausted and needing some rest, he explained to his mother that the insurance would take care of everything as his aunt looked on. She listened to everything that he said before interrupting him, "Dante, have you ever thought about giving up the lifestyle you are living?"

"Where did that come from?"

"Hush child. Listen to me for a second."

"Go ahead, ma."

"Look at you! You have a family and things are going well for you. And I love all my grandchildren, but how do you think Maria feels about the different women? Have you ever asked yourself how she and your other children's mothers feel about your safety?"

"But ma . . ."

"No, no, Dante, don't interrupt me. You don't have to worry about me, I'm fine. You have done a lot for me over the years, but the family is worried about you. We all feel the same way about you, son. I know you're a grown man. However, there isn't a day that goes by that I don't think about your safety, just think about what I'm saying, son."

"I will ma, believe me. I will. I think I'll head home now. I'll talk to you later, ma, Aunt Shelly, take care."

After kissing and hugging his mother and aunt, he headed to his car. And as he drove across the George Washington Bridge, he thought about the things his mother said. He figured she and Maria must have talked about it. Yet, he felt she had no right telling him how to live his life and who to sleep with. He was upset and angry, but she was his mother and he loved her.

EPISODE 11

Five days later . . .

As the sun began to give way to the nightlife, Black and his crew were preparing to take on Big Jeff and his goons, who in a short time had made a name for themselves. He was in a somber mood as he removed two M16 high-powered weapons, two shotguns, and three Glock nine millimeters from the main stash house closet.

"Yo, fellas, let's go! It's time to take care of business," he said. He had a serious look on his face.

They headed down the stairs. Their pulses and heart rates were at a heightened pace. Their adrenalin level was off the Richter. Their throats were dry as their steps quickened, aware of the possibility that some of them may not make it back.

Nonetheless, this didn't hinder nor deter them. The men were quite aware of the job they had to do, and they were going to complete it, no matter what. While they walked to the two black Infiniti Q45s that were parked on the block, Speedy and Black made eye contact. They nodded their heads and touched fists.

There wasn't a murmur in either car as they rolled across the Willis Avenue Bridge into the Bronx. The silence was frightening. They were stoic. They were looking straight ahead with their heads rocking back and forth, as the cars headed up Third Avenue.

Several members of Big Jeff's crew were chilling on the corner with their car radios blasting. Oblivious to the constant flow of traffic passing by, they were getting weeded up as they laughed and clowned each other when several cars pulled up on the corner of East One Hundred and Eightieth Street and Hughes Avenue.

Blaze, Riff, and Suzy alighted from one of the cars and crossed on the opposite side of One Hundred and Eightieth Street. Speedy and Black walked toward Hughes Avenue in the direction of East One Hundred and Eighty-First Street. They turned right onto Belmont Avenue, where they saw four members of Big Jeff's crew having a conversation with several young women. They slowly approached the group.

"Y'all see that nigga?" Black asked.

"Nah. He ain't out here," Riff replied.

"A'ight. See those cats right there, the ones kicking it with those bitches?"

"Yeah," the others replied.

"Do them first. Then we'll take out that other group."

"A'ight," the men said.

Black and his boys were creeping closer when a young "wannabe" member of the Webster Avenue crew sensed that something was wrong. Instead of alerting his boys, he reached for his weapon. Huge mistake, all hell broke loose as gunshots and piercing screams filled the Belmont Avenue block.

Hit multiple times in the head and face, the impact threw the young "wannabe" against an old gray station wagon, and he fell flat on his face onto the concrete pavement. Seeing this, the other group of men returned fire. The block was paralyzed from the rapid sound of gunfire as people scampered.

Two crew members tried in vain to haul ass by blasting away at Blaze and Riff. The men failed in their attempt as they were cornered in the vestibule of one of the buildings where they were cut down in a fusillade of bullets. Wounded and crying, the women ran inside Paro's grocery store and the owner called the police. They had wounds to their legs, back and arms. Black and his boys were racing back to their rides when he realized Suzy was missing.

"Damn! Did anyone see, Suzy?" he screamed.

"Yeah. I saw him," Speedy answered his eyes navigating the block. "He looked a'ight to me if that's what you wanna know."

"Are you sure?" Black insisted, quickly getting into the ride.

"No doubt."

"A'ight, fellas, let's go!" he said in a commanding voice. "If he didn't get hit, he knows his way outta here. So, let's get the fuck up outta this bitch! Yo, Speedy, you sure he was a'ight when you saw him?"

"Yeah, I'm sure! Yo, I ain't see nothin' strange or anything like that."

"Hmm," Black said, glancing through the rear-view mirror as the patrol cars and ambulances with their sirens blasting sped by. He was deeply concerned as the Infinities sped down One Hundred and Eightieth Street toward Webster Avenue. Black was beside himself as he and the crew eagerly waited for whatever information his contact would provide once they got back to Harlem.

"Damn! Still nothin'?" Black said to no one in particular reaching for his cell. He called Maria and told her he would be home late. He never mentioned a word about what had unfolded.

"How could you?" Maria shouted at him.

"How could I what?" he asked with a look of dismay on his face.

"What took you so long to call? I've been hitting you and Suzy for the past three hours and neither of you returned my fucking calls. That's fucked up! Why are you acting like that?"

"I'm sorry, babes. My phone was in the car, and I was discussing business with a few of my people, and you know how that is. I'm sorry. I don't know what happened to Suzy's phone, but he's a'ight. He's taking care of some business for me, don't worry. I'll have him call as soon as I hear from him; I'll talk to you later."

"Don't play with me."

"I'm not babes. I'll have him call you and I'll get back to you."

"Okay, babes." Within minutes of hanging up the phone, his contact filled him in on Suzy's whereabouts.

"He's at St. Barnabas hospital and he's under arrest, he's going to be alright though," Woody said.

"You're sure?" Black asked, still not convinced.

"He was hit in the leg. But like I said, he'll be alright. What? You don't believe me?"

"It's not that, Woody," he said, gesturing to the others that Suzy was alive.

"I'll tell you this though. His ass is in some serious shit," Woody remarked in an unconcerned voice.

It was only later that Black learned that after getting shot, Suzy became delirious while making his getaway. Scared and in shock, he panicked and bolted through the elementary school yard at the corner of East One Hundred and Eightieth Street and Belmont Avenue.

His eyes were wide open as the cool night breeze hit his dry lips. He took a deep breath as he ran up Crotona Avenue and headed toward Tremont Avenue. The police sirens were blaring as he dragged his bloody leg across the street. He slowed down as he got to the corner of Tremont Avenue. His heart was pounding as sweat began pouring from his forehead. As he limped through the intersection, three patrol cars veered down on him and cornered him.

"Get down mutha-fucka! On the fucking ground, keep your fucking hands where I can see them!" the officers screamed with their guns drawn.

"I'm down! I'm down!" Suzy yelled fearing for his life, his voice cracking.

"Where is the gun mutha-fucka? Where is it?" they demanded as they quickly cuffed him.

"I ain't got a gun! I ain't got nothin'!" Suzy cried out as the officers pulled him to his feet and searched him.

Seeing that he didn't have a weapon, the officers put him in their patrol car, only to hear one of their partners scream, "We found a gun! We found a gun!"

"Oh! You tossed the shit away, huh?" one of the officers barked.

"I don't know what you talking about, that ain't mine. That shit is not mine!" Suzy proclaimed as they removed him to an awaiting ambulance.

Black was relieved that Suzy wasn't dead. He would have had a lot to explain to Maria. He was more worried about whether or not they would link Suzy and the crew to the triple murder, and the innocent people who were shot. The thought of Suzy cooperating and informing on the crew was what troubled him the most. After giving it some thought, he called Maria and told her what happened. Shocked and dismayed, Maria listened to what he was saying, and though she was worried, he told her to remain calm. After composing herself, she agreed with him that things would work out fine.

"Just do me a favor, baby?" Maria said in a distraught voice.

"What's that boo?"

"Will you return my calls even if it's just to say that you're, okay?"

"I will."

"Please, don't keep me in the dark?" she begged.

"Baby, you right, I won't do it again. I love you, girl."

"I love you too, babes."

***

The city was in turmoil. The backlash from the police department's inaction led to a shockwave of demonstrations throughout the city. The department was trying its best to calm the community's fear. Only then did they turn up the heat on the dealers. The police were now on a mission. They were swift and decisive. The action which the department took didn't fare too well for several rogue officers, either. They had to watch their backs, fearing that one of their own might turn on them, thus they kept a low profile. The New York newspapers highlighted the killings on their front pages. One paper's front page read: *'Three killed and three wounded in Bronx Shooting.'*

Black was not satisfied, despite taking out three of Big Jeff's minions. He wanted Big Jeff dead and he promised himself, he would not stop until he was. He was also upset with Woody, who took more than half of the one-hundred grand and hadn't delivered. He had some remorse after the death of Riff's, cousin. He blamed himself for not taking out Half Pint when he had the opportunity.

Maybe Daryl would still be alive, he thought to himself, vowing never to let anyone who crossed him and deserved to die, escape his grasp. When he received news that Peaches was found naked, bound, and shot to death, he turned and point a finger at Speedy and said, "Bitches like that ain't worth a damn! She was fucking you, right, Speedy?"

"No doubt."

"Then look what she did. She set that pussy ass nigga, Half. And then turned around and started fucking Low. Do you think she didn't know what she was doing? She was going hard body. That bitch was grimey!"

"Word, Black! That's why I left that bitch alone," he said. "Who knows? That bitch probably would have set me too."

"Believe me that shit was coming. I told you about fucking with those chicken heads and project chicks."

"That shit is a rap. I know what time it is," he nodded, making his point.

"Stay clear of those bitches, y'all."

"Word," Speedy and Riff replied, nodding in agreement.

***

The wire was hot, as word got out that the Syndicate was involved in the Bronx killings and several crews made some disparaging comments. Black would have none of it, as he sent the crews a message telling them to stay out of his affairs, and Trigga was more than ready to defend him.

"That's what's up, Black, we ain't no fucking sample for mutha-fuckas to disrespect. If it's a war, it's a war if it's peace, it's peace!" Trigga said with a screw face.

"This is how it's supposed to be, son."

"For real, you have to put fear in a mutha-fucka's heart."

"Word, I have to let these mutha-fuckas know the Syndicate is not to be fucked with!"

"True that. But what's up with that thing you were telling me about?"

"It's still in the works; I'll let you know."

"When."

"Just link me."

"Waddup with Adiba? It's been a while since I last saw her."

Laughing, he said, "She cool still. She's just doing her thing with school and all that."

"Tell her I said hi."

"I got you."

"Just link me and let me know what's up with that thing."

"A'ight, Trigga."

EPISODE 12

It was a cool and brisk evening as Black drove south, passing the Crystal Lounge on Lenox and One Hundred and Twenty-Third Street. The Crystal, a renowned bar and lounge catered to many of the old-timers in the community. And as he made a left turn onto One Hundred and Twenty-Second Street, he immediately began taking notice of the street-lined brownstones.

He had driven by on numerous occasions but never paid particular attention to the row of brownstones with their three and four-story structures. He was taken aback by the serene silence of the street, only the barking of a dog from a third-story roof interrupted the quietness. His mind was elsewhere as he noticed a cat asleep in a window. An elderly man wearing a white fedora sits on the stoop of a brownstone smoking a cigar. Black smiled at the old-timer who never looked his way. *Buying one of these brownstones would be a great investment,* he thought.

And as he approached the red light on the corner of Fifth Avenue, a tall slim man with salt and pepper hair ran toward his car. Startled for a moment, he soon realized it was Joe's drinking buddy, Barry. Barry was in a state of shock outside the Crystal Lounge when Black drove by. Yet he had the wherewithal to chase after the car when he saw that Black wasn't going to stop.

A look of panic and horror was on his face as he yelled, "Black, they just shot Joe-Joe inside the Crystal, he's dead."

"What?" he said, with a stunned look on his face, pulling over and getting out of the car. "What the fuck happened?"

Black and Barry began walking the two blocks to the Crystal.

"He got into an argument with some cats from Sugar Hill. And a big nigga name Frank shot him several times," Barry stuttered.

"Fuck!" he said aloud.

Joe's body was lying on the floor of the lounge as the police cars pulled up. Black walked outside, pulled out his cell, and called his mother and aunt.

"Barry, what happened?" he asked, clearly distraught.

"Me, Joe-Joe, and Denise were having a drink when Frank made a pass at Denise," he said, shaken.

"Who was Denise with you or Joe-Joe?"

"She was with Joe. Joe told Frank that's his woman. Frank got pissed."

"What did he say?"

"He said, 'I don't give a fuck whose woman she is. Mind your fucking business, punk.' I told Joe let's leave, but he wouldn't listen. The next thing I know a bunch of niggas from Sugar Hill was in his face. He tried to run, but Frank pulled out a gun and shot him."

While Barry and Black spoke, his mother and aunt arrived. A distraught Black was speechless as they approached him. Panic-stricken and filled with grief, they stared at their brother's body in disbelief.

"Give me a second, ma," he said, getting on the phone. He called Speedy. Within minutes, Speedy arrived.

"Are you okay, ma? Aunt Shelly, you, okay?" he asked them, as the body was being removed.

"Yes, Dante," both women replied fighting back their tears.

"Hi, Mrs. Reynolds. Hi, Ms. Shelly," Speedy greeted them.

"Hello, Cory," they both responded.

"I'm sorry about what happened," he said. "Thank you, Cory."

"What did the cops say?" Black asked his mother and aunt.

"Well, they know who did it, and they have several witnesses including Barry, who gave statements and are willing to do so in court. One of the officers said the guy who did it will be arrested later tonight," Shelly said.

"Good, so where do we go from here?" he asked, putting his arm around them.

"We have to go down to the morgue first. I guess we'll go home after that, and start making funeral arrangements," Mrs. Reynolds said sadly.

"I've got it, don't worry about the money."

"Okay, son."

"Does Ray know?" Black wanted to know.

"No, Raymond doesn't know. We're gonna stop by his mother's apartment later," Shelly said.

"Go ahead and do that ma, I'll call you later. Aunt Shelly, talk to you later."

"Be careful, Dante," his mother said, hugging him.

"I will ma," he said in a sad voice.

"Cory, take care," both women said.

"You too," Speedy said. He hugged them. Raymond, the eldest of Joe's two children with his ex-wife, lived in Harlem with other relatives. The family was concerned about how he would respond to his father's death. They kept their eyes on him throughout the whole ordeal, and despite the tears, he shed at the funeral, they all admired his resiliency. Joe was given a wonderful send-off, and his body was interred in Heavenly Peace Cemetery in the Bronx. As for Frank, he was arrested and charged with Joe's murder. The men who were with Frank cooperated and testified against him in court, and he was sentenced to twenty-five years to life.

***

Big Jeff's new second in command, was a Panamanian by the name of Shrug. He was manipulative, calculating, cold-hearted, and a vicious killer. Aware of this, Black cautioned his crew repeatedly. While Big Jeff and his goons discussed their next move, some members of the crew were screaming revenge. Big Jeff and Shrug assured them it would only be a matter of time before they strike back at the Syndicate. Knowing the war could go on for years, Black knew it could negatively affect his business, and this he was mindful of.

Black retained a high-powered lawyer for Suzy, who was locked up in the hospital infirmary on Rikers Island. He was charged with three counts of murder, three counts of attempted murder, and numerous other charges. He was visited by a couple of detectives who tried their best to intimidate and threaten him to tell on the crew. He knew what they were up to and refused to budge as their visits became more frequent.

"Fuck that shit! I ain't a snitch!" Suzy told the detectives whenever they visited.

Maria visited him every other weekend and made sure he had a package and money in his commissary. She kept him updated on the operations of the business, the family, and the old neighborhood. But more importantly, she reassured him that he had Black's support. Suzy felt a whole lot better hearing those words. They were a source of comfort, despite the charges he faced.

With Suzy out of the picture, Blaze took his position as the number three man in the organization. He was in charge of all operations in the Bronx. Well-loved, and respected by the customers, he single-handedly ignited a major recruiting drive for the organization. While their membership grew, Black began noticing that Blaze was making a lot of rash decisions and getting involved with a few questionable women. He knew this sort of behavior was not good for business.

"Yo, Blaze, I think you need to slow down a bit," Black suggested, knowing he would brush him off.

"What do you mean?"

"You know, the girls, the decisions you make. Sometimes things' ain't really what they seem. You need to check some of the girls you roll with. I think they fucking with your decision-making skills."

"Alright, Black."

"Cool," he replied, knowing everything went in one ear and came out the other.

Blaze was angry that he was interfering in his private life. However, Black could care less about his women and what he did when he wasn't on the clock. The only thing that mattered to him was his money. And Blaze's behavior was troubling to not only him, but to the rank and file of the organization. As uncooperative as he was when Black first approached him, he eventually relented to his warning and slowed his antics down. However, it was short-lived, and in no time, he was back to his old antics.

***

"I don't know why this young mutha-fucka keeps sweating me," Blaze expressed to several young girls he was hanging out with.

"Maybe he's jealous because you're the man," one of the girls quipped, having no idea that Blaze worked for Black.

Hyping and flossing were some of the guises Blaze used to sway his coop of undesirables into believing he was the man, and not knowing any better, they believed him. They would hang out with him in the drug houses. He took them on many of his runs, counting thousands of dollars in front of them, and pretending the money belonged to him. Several of the girls were smoking and he wasn't aware of it. When it was brought to his attention, he dismissed it as nonsense. Nonetheless, a few weeks later, Speedy reminded him that Black wasn't too pleased.

"It's all a bunch of bullshit, Speedy! They're not smoking," he tried to convince him.

"You sure?"

"Don't you think if they were smoking, I would know about it?"

"Look, Blaze! I fucks with you 'cause you a cool mutha-fucka, but Im'a keep it real with you. Black ain't feeling all this drama."

"Me and Black spoke about this before," Blaze said, somewhat apprehensive.

"And what did he say?"

"He told me to check my girls, and I did."

"Yo, I'm telling you for your own good, son. Some of those bitches are hitting the pipe right under your nose."

"Says who, you, Speedy? Go ahead with that shit. I'm a grown-ass man; I don't need all this shit."

"You know what, Blaze?"

"What?"

"You need to slow that shit down, son. You in fucking denial, I'm out."

"Yeah, okay," he replied incensed with a bit of sarcasm in his voice. *I don't know why he's listening to that Jamaican mutha-fucka. They killed his fucking uncle, and he didn't do shit, and this dumb mutha-fucka is listening to him. Fuck them niggas*! He said to himself.

Blaze was more upset at himself than anything else. Not only was he smoking, but he also feared being found out. However, he would soon realize what everyone was saying about the girls who visited one night. No sooner than they arrived they bought a twenty-dollar piece of crack cocaine. Blaze was taken aback, as they pulled out their crack pipes. He couldn't believe his eyes as he stood there watching them. He was tempted as they blazed their pipes in his face. It didn't take long before they were paranoid and begging for another hit.

"Y'all, know you have to take care of me, first, right?" Blaze said smiling.

There wasn't any shame in the girl's game as they began sucking his dick. Caught up in the threesome, Blaze fucked and sucked the girls as he bathed in pussy heaven. Intoxicated from both pussies, he pulled out his crack pipe and joined them. Tired of the constant ringing of the doorbell, and lost in his stupor of sex and crack, he told the customers that he was out of product.

Within minutes, every crack head within a 25- yard radius was alerted, angry and upset. Pussy and ass were all that mattered to Blaze, and he was having the time of his life, as they smoked their way into a drug bliss.

At the rate that he was going, and the constant complaints from the customers, it didn't take long before word got back to Black and the others about his foolhardiness and reckless behavior. Black watched the madness unfold as his behavior became more and more erratic. Money and drugs were also missing from the daily payroll. And whenever the opportunity presented itself, the girls would steal hundreds of dollars. And although he would make it up out of his pocket, with his lying-ass self, Black was livid.

Days later . . .

Black felt he had put too much time into organizing the Syndicate. And he wasn't going to let the whole operation go down because of Blaze's stupidity. He had to make a decision and a decisive one at that.

"What's the deal with Blaze?" Riff asked, one evening as the men sat around talking.

"He's fucking up!" Bee exclaimed. "My boy is fucking up!"

"Damn!" Black said, dejected. "I tried talking to him, but he won't listen. I fucks with that nigga 'cause he was my uncle's man, but this shit has to stop."

"He's smoking that shit with them chicken heads. All those bitches from the projects got his ass open. Enough is enough!" Speedy snapped.

"We're losing a lot of paper, and it doesn't make any sense. He's my man and all, but this is ridiculous," Fats chimed in.

"Hmm," Black said tapping his fingers on the table. When the final decision was made, there was some ambiguity amongst them in deciding who would carry out the hit. Seeing the indecisiveness, Black took matters into his own hands.

***

The next day . . .

It was a Saturday night. It was raining. He could hear the patter of rain hitting the roof of his car, and as he pulled up, it began pouring heavily. He thought about waiting for it to ease up but changed his mind just as quickly. Taking several quick strides as the rain and wind whipped across his face, he quickly made his way to the building. Hearing the knock on the door, Blaze peered through the peephole, and seeing it was Black, he told him to wait a second.

"Sure, take your time," he replied, emotionless as music blared from inside the apartment.

Entering the apartment, the aroma of crack mixed with Lysol spray greeted him. Blaze was sweating profusely, licking his lips, and acting jittery. Black walked into the living room. Sitting at the kitchen table was an attractive young girl. No older than twenty, she was the mother of a five-year-old boy, and a crack head, but she kept herself well-groomed. Sitting next to her was the young girl, who thought highly of Blaze. Taking a seat on one of the couches, Black asked how much product and money was in the house. Blaze handed him half a kilo of cocaine and five grand.

"Yo, you sure that's it?" he asked.

"Yeah, that's it, Speedy and Riff came by and took twenty-five grand and left me with this."

"Yeah. I know about that," he said in a rather soft voice. "How much have you sold since?"

"About five grand."

Black knew he was lying. The spot was selling eleven grand easily, and on the weekends, even more, despite his closing it down whenever he gets into his sexual trysts with his women. He knew he was pocketing at least five grand a day from the profit. Getting up from her seat, the loud mouth girl walked over to Blaze and asked, "Who this dude, and why is he asking all these questions?" Black overheard her saying. He remained calm.

He knew Blaze had been playing him, and as he continued with the questions, his responses weren't making any sense. Pissed, he didn't like the body language or the tone of Black's questions as he stared at the girls. The young mother looked uncomfortable. Her friend's body language resonated as if she wanted Blaze to challenge Black. He could tell Blaze was questioning himself. He saw the discomfort and fear on his face. Blaze began pacing. One minute he was sitting and the next minute he was up, trying to explain that everything was fine.

"So, what about you, are you okay?" Black asked, trying to keep him cool.

"Yeah. I'm alright," he stuttered, with a worried look on his face.

"You got anything to drink?" Black asked, staring into the eyes of the young mother and her loudmouth friend.

"Yeah. I've got some beer."

"Let me get one," he said, getting up from the couch.

"A'ight."

Blaze opened the refrigerator door and snatched up two bottles of Heineken. He handed one to Black. He was about to close the door when a shot rang out, Boom! Blood and flesh splattered on the interior and exterior of the refrigerator. Blaze crumbled to the floor like a piece of paper as the young mother and her friend stood there momentarily stunned; before screaming at the top of their lungs.

Their screams didn't deter Black, as he fired a round into the young mother's forehead. She fell backward with her eyes wide open. Pleading that she wanted to pee, the loudmouth sister knew her chances of getting out of her situation were second to none. Black deliberately left her for last. With a scowl on his face, he calmly said, "I'm the boss, not him, bye!" Loud enough so she could hear, before firing two rounds in her forehead, the slugs ripped into her brain knocking her off the chair. He coolly placed the drugs and money in a bag and pulled the door behind him.

The tenants in the building were so used to hearing gunshots; they paid no attention to the loud noise. Within hours, several workers made their way to the apartment, removed the bodies, and dumped them later that night in Van Cortlandt Park. Losing that drug house would have been a substantial loss for the organization.

EPISODE 13

Black was a drug dealer, plain and simple. He was no different from the dealers who took control of the buildings where they sold their drugs. The decent folks who remained were prisoners in their own homes. Despite the efforts of the police who patrolled the buildings in the daytime, come nightfall, it was a different story. For those who could move, they gladly got their asses out of there. But for those who didn't have the resources to do so, had to deal with the drugs, shootings, and drug addicts.

Black didn't give a damn. He was only interested in making money. If anything or anyone happened to stand between him and his money, they were dealt with. The girls were given a little leeway. They could pay off their debt by having sex, sucking a few dicks, running a few errands out of town, or allowing him to use their apartment.

Their businesses in the mid-west and the south were booming. They were on top of the world. The year 2003 was a good one and heading into 2004, they expected more of the same. Not only had he reopened his mother's business, but he also opened two additional laundromats in Brooklyn, which his aunt and cousin were in charge of. He also opened a restaurant and bar in Manhattan called Stylz, which was operated by Adiba and other family members. The place was elegant, yet trendy. His clientele included celebrities from sports, movies, entertainment, rap, reggae, and the dancehall world.

He loved rubbing shoulders with the celebrities that would show up. Yet he was smart enough to know that if he weren't involved in the drug trade, he wouldn't be catering to such an elite crowd. Thus, he didn't let any of it go to his head. He also enjoyed the ordinary people who showed up week after week. They were his meal ticket. They were the ones he could count on filling the joint. Maria was elated because she believed this was the right kind of project for him. She was willing to wait and see how he would respond after a year in the business. The restaurant and bar were a blessing in disguise for her. Not only was she involved in the daily operations, but she was seeing him a lot more.

Black was more than generous as the rank-and-file gave thousands of dollars to the foot soldiers and their street lookouts. None of this could prevent the violence and bloodshed that his organization was about to suffer. Several members were shot dead by rival drug dealers and others were jailed in North Carolina and Georgia. The body count grew as the Syndicate retaliated. Both sides had their share of fatalities. Black insisted that the crew would only move on his orders. Several of his foot soldiers barked at the idea amongst themselves. They had a problem with this rule. It didn't take long before Speedy found out what was going on. He immediately informed Black, and they were quickly dealt with.

"Nobody and I mean nobody is gonna undermine what we have built!" Black snapped.

"These niggas are slipping," Speedy said to him.

"Listen, here is what you do."

"What?"

"Tell Rasheed to merk any mutha-fucka that ain't following the rules."

"No doubt."

"And tell him to keep me informed."

"A'ight."

The code that he laid out to the crew was simple: abide by, and always respect the hierarchy of the organization. Never use the product. No sleeping around with each other's wives or girlfriends, and the ultimate, never give information on a fellow member. Black was serious about these rules and to enforce them he became more ruthless.

***

Ray stood a slender six-three, with neatly braided cornrows. Dark in complexion, he was very handsome, and even at the tender age of eighteen, he had a loyal following of young girls who were fond of him. Proud of his Jamaican background, he would let others know this in a heartbeat. Young and brash, he was known for blasting dancehall music from his jet-black Audi convertible.

Ray admired the lifestyle his older cousin led, and he wanted to be just like him. Black knew his intention and found himself in an awkward position. He and Ray spoke about joining the organization, but he never gave him a definite answer. He was somewhat apprehensive, and he was worried about what his mother and other family members might say. And he didn't want him to end up like Crip. But after thinking it over, and Ray's constant badgering, he finally gave in, and allowed him to join the organization.

Ray loved partying and hanging out with his girlfriend, Trina, who lived in the Bronx. Trina also loved to party. So, when she invited him to her girlfriend, Latasha's party, he agreed to go. They had been dating for two years after meeting each other through a mutual friend. Trina had no idea that Ray was a member of the Syndicate. He kept that side of his life a secret. He treated her well and she loved it. The party was in the Parkchester section of the Bronx.

Everyone was having a good time when Ray and Trina showed up. They were loud and raucous. The music was pumping. Cigarette and marijuana smoke filled the hallway and apartment. The young women were sexily clad, dressed in tight-fitting outfits as they gyrated their bodies to the pulsating beats. A group of men stood close to the door, leaning against the walls sipping on Cristal, Moet, and Hypnotic.

Ray's eyes began scanning the scantily clad young women as he made his way past them. Trina was stunning looking in a tight-fitting dress. None of this mattered to Ray, it seemed, but the men at the party soon made him aware of it. They thought she was cute, sexy, and hot. Their continuous stares, and him grilling them didn't stop them from watching her every move.

Ray was feeling tipsy after a few drinks. He couldn't keep his eyes off the attractive young girl approaching Trina.

"Hi, Trina!" she said, eyeing Ray.

"Hi," she replied, obviously not happy to see her.

"Who's that? What's his name?" she asked, boldly.

"What the fuck you mean what's his name?" Trina rolled her eyes. "He's with me."

"Girl, I was only playing."

"Yeah, right!"

"Seriously, don't take it like that. You know you, my girl."

"Sure," Trina bristled.

"Aren't you gonna introduce me?" she asked, pryingly.

"Ray, this is Melissa."

"What's up, Melissa? How you doing?" he said.

"I'm fine. You're cute." Ray smiled and nodded his head.

"No, you didn't bitch!" Trina said, pissed off. "You need to stop playing yourself, Melissa."

"All I said was he's cute, daaag."

"Get the fuck outta here bitch!" Trina said, angrily.

"Fuck you, bitch!" Melissa replied, sashaying across the room. Ray couldn't hold back his laughter.

"What the fuck is so funny? Do you think that shit is cute? You smiling up in her face like you like that shit! If you like that shit, then go be with her!"

"I ain't think that shit is funny. And nobody was smiling up in her face. Come on now, what do you mean go be with her, fuck her! I'm with you; it's just that your girl is a snap."

"That bitch is a ho! She's lucky I didn't beat her ass. I don't know why Latasha invited her skank ass," Trina said, as Melissa walked by with her eyes on Ray.

Ray thought she was cute, but he knew better than to say that to Trina, who was still upset at him for acting a fool.

"Come on baby, let's get our groove on." He pulled her close.

"I don't want your dick rubbing all on me." She giggled. "Maybe you wanna give it to that nasty ho."

Laughing, Ray said, "Fuck that bitch! She ain't got nothin' on you, babes!"

"For real?" she asked in a soft sexy baby voice.

"Yeah, for real," he smiled, looking her in the face, biting his bottom lip.

Ray and Trina were doing their thing as the deejay kept hitting the crowd with all the latest joints. Melissa kept staring at him as she danced with a busted-looking brother, whom she kept at a distance, as her breast bounced in sync with her gyrating hips. Her eyes were focused on Ray as she teasingly licked her lips, knowing she had his full attention. Trina, whose back was turned didn't see a thing.

"I'll be right back, okay. Im'a get something to drink. You need anything?" Ray asked.

"No. I'm cool," Trina said, taking a seat in the corner of the room.

As Ray headed toward the back of the room, Trina lost sight of him. He was standing by the kitchen when he noticed Melissa walking toward him. "Ray!" she said. "Do you wanna come in the bedroom and smoke an L with me?"

"Hell, yeah, this one is on me!" he said excitedly, reaching in his top pocket.

He was a player. He knew the game, and he knew what she wanted. He wasn't about to disappoint her. He knew she was horny as they entered the bedroom.

"That shit smells good, let me get a hit," she said in a sexy voice.

"No doubt," he replied, handing it to her as he anticipated how he was going to fuck her. Giggling as she took several quick puffs, Ray began feeling on her breast. She opened her blouse giving him full access. He bit and sucked her tits.

"Yeah!" she moaned, as she puffed on the blunt. She began rubbing his dick as she pulled him closer.

"Pass that shit!" Ray said, taking three quick puffs. "What's up with the pussy? Are you gonna let a nigga hit it or what?"

She didn't say a word as he pushed her up against the wall and began groping her. His time was limited, and he had to make this a quickie. She stroked his dick as he pulled his zipper down while reaching in his wallet for a condom. They kissed long and hard. He caressed her soft breast while he fingered her pussy. As he pulled her pants down, he noticed she wasn't wearing any panties. He became even more aroused as he slid on the condom. He slid his dick in her wet pussy and began fucking her slowly.

Trina was worried as she walked toward the front door and looked in the hallway. She then walked to the back, but only got as far as the kitchen before she was told the bedrooms were off-limits. As she headed back toward the living room, a female friend of Melissa said, "You know the guy you came with?"

"Yeah, what about him?"

"He drove off about fifteen minutes ago with some chick."

"Are you serious?"

"Yeah. I just saw him."

"A'ight." Trina was baffled. She called his cell phone and got his voicemail.

Why the fuck would he leave without telling me? I didn't see his ass leave. Fuck! I don't believe that shit! But where the fuck is he? Damn, Ray! Trina said to herself.

Meanwhile, Ray was indulging in his self-gratification. "Ah, Melissa moaned. You do it good, gimme some slow wine. Yeah, just like that!"

"Yeah. You like it?" he asked, gripping her ass.

"Uh-uh. Your dick feels good. Uh, uh, uh, right there! Don't stop! Oh, yeah! Right there! Hit it, Ray!"

"Like this?" he said as he slowly worked his dick in and out of her.

"Yeah, like that! Take off the condom."

"Nah. I ain't with that!" He objected.

"No, take it off and let me suck your dick."

"Oh, a'ight, cool."

She was sucking it like a professional. Her head was bobbing up and down as she held his hard dick in her mouth. Her tongue glided over his shaft buckling his knees as his dick kept hitting the corners of her mouth. They were both in a delirious state of ecstasy. They barely heard the knock on the door. Standing at the door was Melissa's friend, Tyesha.

She called Melissa aside and whispered in her ears. Ray had a gut feeling that something was wrong, but he felt whatever it was, it didn't concern him. His only concern was explaining himself to Trina about his whereabouts.

After Tyesha left the room, Melissa coaxed him into bed. She screamed as he fucked her. Luckily, the music drowned out her screams. Ray was oblivious to anything else that was taking place around him. His only concern was Melissa.

He never saw the masked gunman who entered the room. What he saw was a shotgun staring him in the face and Melissa with a vexed look on her face. Two blasts from the shotgun tore into his face as flesh and blood splattered against the wall, sheets, and floor. He was in severe pain as a horrific wail for help reverberated inside the bedroom, and then silence. Ray's blood-soaked body was still. The killer then removed his mask and jumped out the window onto the fire escape.

The music stopped. People were screaming. Trina, hearing the shots, felt something tugging at her insides as she ran to the bedroom. The smell of gun powder and a slight marijuana scent filled the room. Blood was everywhere as she got closer and saw that it was Ray. She lost it. She screamed at the top of her lungs. The blood from the sheets and Ray's body were on her clothes. She held his head sobbing. The place was in chaos. People were scrambling to get out of the apartment. The hit man hurried across the street along with the fleeing mob. He got in the passenger side seat of a blue Range Rover with its engine roaring and sped towards Tremont Avenue.

"Did you do that nigga?" Tyesha asked, anticipating an answer.

"Yeah. That puta won't be seeing Black tonight." The hitman smiled.

Trina was hysterical and screaming as she kept muttering over and over again, "Why did they kill him? Why? Why?"

Her friends tried to comfort her as Melissa, always the actress sat on the edge of the bed shedding crocodile tears. Trina, in shock, didn't say a word as the hurt and pain took control of her emotions.

"Who got shot?" asked the busted-looking guy who had danced with Melissa earlier.

"Who did it?" Trina's friend Donna inquired.

"Oh, shit, it's Ray!" Latasha gasped in shock.

The look on the faces of those who either saw the killer when he entered the party or when he left was one of shock and disbelief.

***

Hours later . . .

"Yo, Riff," Hutch, a local wannabe thug who was always hanging around the crew called out.

"Waddup, son?"

"You heard about that shit?"

"What shit?"

"The shooting!"

"Nah. Where did that happen?"

"In the Bronx, up in Parkchester, they merked some young cat at a party."

"Word! Who the kid that got shot?"

"I don't know, but the word on the wire is that it's some kid from Harlem. They said some bitch set him up."

"When this shit happened, son?" he asked, seemingly concerned. He knew Ray was hanging out in the Bronx.

"Tonight! A few hours ago."

"Word? A'ight!" He had a strange feeling as he walked to his car. His gut feeling was to contact Black, but he felt he needed more information before doing so until his phone rang.

"What's up?" he answered.

"Yo, Ray got shot up in the Bronx," the caller said.

"Ah, fuck! Damn, man! Is he okay?"

"Nah son, he's dead."

"Fuck! Does Black know?"

"He should by now. Meet us at One Hundred and Sixteenth."

Black was devastated. He was at a loss for words. Allowing Ray to join the organization had backfired. Would his family blame him? How would he explain Ray's death to his mother? He was in deep thought. He was transfixed on the reality that his cousin was no longer alive, and the rank and file of the organization was awaiting his next move.

The next day . . .

"Did anyone talk to Trina?" Black asked.

"Nah," Speedy answered.

"Somebody needs to get her ass over here, or on the phone."

"Yo, let me hit this girl up and see if I can get her number."

Black was still trying to make sense of what happened when Speedy handed him his phone.

"Hi, Trina, this is Ray's cousin, Black."

"Hi."

"You may not know me, but I have heard a lot about you."

"Whatever you heard I hope it was good," she said in a refreshed tone despite her grief.

"Absolutely! It was all good. Ray never said a bad word about you," he responded, hearing the warmth in her voice.

"Okay. You're his big cuz, right? And your sister's name is Adiba?"

"You got it. That's right," he said, smiling. Trina explained everything and told him Melissa's whereabouts. He thanked her.

"No problem," Trina cried.

"I'll let you know when and where the wake and the funeral will be."

"Okay," she softly murmured. He felt a lot of remorse for Trina as he hung up the phone. Nonetheless, he was grateful for the information. Turning to Speedy, he said, "Find that bitch!"

***

The next day, Big Jeff and his crew were having lunch at Mama's Sweet Soul Food and Caribbean Restaurant. It was a regular hangout for many of the players and dealers, including Black and his crew. Divine and Trigga also frequented the place. Despite the constant threat of death, Big Jeff, Shrug, and several of Black's sworn enemies were also regulars.

Numerous shootings had taken place over the years; luckily, no one was ever killed. One would think that a troubled eatery where death loomed would have been shut down by now. Instead, it remained the favorite of many not only in Harlem but throughout the other boroughs.

On this particular day, Jeff and his partners were discussing business and Ray's death.

"Yo! That bitch had it coming to him anyway, good for that mutha-fucka! All those niggas including his big bad cousin, uncle, whatever that nigga is to him, they all going down! Let me ask y'all this, who did the shit? And wasn't it a bitch who set him up? Black is probably going out of his fucking mind right now," Big Jeff snickered, as the others laughed.

Getting serious, Shrug said to Big Jeff, "See, we can't afford to let these bitches get in our way. It was a bitch that set his mutha-fucking ass up. There are only three kinds of women a mutha-fucka should want in his life. His mother, his daughter, and his woman, that's it! You respect your mother; you love your daughter, and you fuck your woman. That's it, everyone else is a bitch. They are nada, nothin'! And never let any of these grimey bitches get close, or your asses will end up like Ray, especially in this game," he sternly warned.

"That's what I'm talking about, I hope y'all niggas take a page out of Shrug's book," Big Jeff remarked.

Several days later, Ray's funeral was held at Antioch Baptist Church in Harlem. The place was filled as family and friends came to pay their respect.

"They did a wonderful job on his face. At least he had an open coffin," Shelly said.

"Yes, they did," Mrs. Reynolds concurred. "It would have been a shame if we hadn't gotten to see his face one last time. God bless him. At least he's with his father now."

There wasn't a dry eye in the place. Trina, who was sobbing, had to be restrained when Ray's coffin was closed for the trip to the cemetery.

"When is it gonna stop?" Ray's mother screamed, as his coffin was placed in its final resting place.

"Lord help us!" Mrs. Reynolds wailed.

"This has to stop, Jennifer! They are killing each other for what? Oh, God! Look at my son! My poor son!" Ray's mother cried as she rested her head on Mrs. Reynold's shoulder. Black had a scowl on his face as he observed the pain etched on his family's faces.

"Ashes to ashes, dust to dust," the pastor said, as those in attendance slowly laid a flower on top of Ray's coffin, as it slowly descended into the earth next to his father. While several grim-faced officers watched the whole thing unfold, Black and Speedy kept their eyes on them.

EPISODE 14

"Hi, Dante!" a faint voice said, as he looked over his right shoulder to see where the voice was coming from. Standing online in Mama's Sweet Soul Food and Caribbean Restaurant, his roving eyes quickly spotted the person who called his name. Sitting at a table for two with his long legs extended was a tall, slender, middle-aged man with salt and pepper hair. His face was wrinkled, haggard, and drawn. He had bloodshot eyes and discolored pink and black lips. As he got closer, there was a strong stench of alcohol emanating from him. In his top left breast pocket was a small bottle of Smirnoff Vodka. His huge hands and fingers were filled with dirt.

"What do you want?" Black asked. He had a look of disdain on his face.

"I'm sorry to bother you, but I wanted to know."

"Know what?"

"Nothing, son!"

"Son? You got the nerves to call me, son? What right do you have to call me son, tell me?"

Taken aback and visibly shaken from Black's attitude towards him, he was at a loss for words.

"I thought that . . ."

"You thought what? You thought you could roll upon me and say hi, and everything would be cool? You didn't even ask me how mom and Adiba are doing."

"You never gave me the chance. I was about to ask, but you cut me off."

"They both cool, no thanks to you. I bet you didn't even know that Joe-Joe and Lil Ray is dead?"

"Yeah. I heard. Some of the old-timers were talking about it. But I couldn't make it to the funerals. What would I look like showing up after all these years? Who would accept me? Would you? Would your mother? Who would, Dante?"

"You could have still shown up. It was about paying your respect. We all family in case you didn't know, but I guess an old dog can never change. You a fucking bastard! Why the fuck don't you go back to Jamaica since you ain't got no family here?"

Stunned by the ire and tone of Black's language, he was about to walk out of the restaurant forgetting his lady friend, when a female voice interrupted them, "Who the fuck is this, Willy?" a short, brown-skinned woman asked, as she slithered her big ass into the seat next to him.

"Shut up, Yvonne!" he said, glaring at her. "This doesn't concern you."

"You wanna know who the fuck I am? Who the fuck are you?" Black snapped, as she quickly turned her attention to Willy.

"Don't tell me to shut up, Willy. Who the fuck is he, and what the fuck does he want? You gonna let him talk to me like that?"

"Stay out of this, it's none of your business!" he snapped.

"And why you telling me it's none of my business, I just wanna know what the fuck is going on!" she continued with an attitude.

Willy was about to respond when Black cut him off, "I'm his son, that's who the fuck I am!" Black said it in a calm but stern tone.

There was a slight smile on his father's face, but it quickly faded as Black continued,

"He walked out on my mother and sister. I guess he left us alone to be with a loudmouth, alcoholic low life bitch like you. That's what's up! Anything else you wanna know, bitch?" he asked sarcastically, as the other patrons in the restaurant turned to see where the commotion was coming from.

Yvonne was staring at him with her mouth wide open. She then turned to Willy and whispered in his ear, "Is he your son?"

"Yes, he is. Why?"

"This is the guy I was telling you about, the dealer. I remember his face. I think they call him Blake or Black, something like that. It's his shit we be buying around the way. See if you can get some shit from him."

Willy's mind was working overtime as he contemplated how he would ask the question. Black paid him no attention as he stood at the counter ordering his food.

"Can I talk to you for a minute outside?" Willy mumbled as he approached him.

"What do you want?"

"Are you a drug dealer, and do they call you, Black, son?"

"What? Yeah, me sell drugs. And what the fuck is it to you? And don't call me son, I ain't your mutha-fucking, son. My name is, Dante, and yeah, they call me, Black! Why? What's it to you?" he barked at him.

"I was wondering if you could give your old man a few dollars." Black thought he would have been upset that he was a drug dealer, instead, he was asking for money.

"Bloodclaat! Well, ain't this a bitch?" Black chuckled.

It certainly didn't make any sense for him to tell Yvonne that he was his son and in the same breath admonish him for calling him so. Yet, this was the type of person he was. This was another way of suppressing his anger, instead of compounding the bitterness that he felt towards him.

Acting out verbally made more sense to him than resorting to violence against his father. Black stared at him. He was angry that the only thing that seemed to matter to him was his money. Inquiring about the family was not on his agenda. The only thing he was worried about was getting high.

After all these years, he's still the same; he's the same irresponsible punk-ass mutha-fucka. He'll never change, Black thought to himself.

While he contemplated his father's disparaging behavior and how he abandoned them, he reached into his pocket and pulled out a knot of cash and threw it on the sidewalk.

"Go ahead, take that, and stay the fuck away from us! You have been in Harlem all this time and not once did you visit. But you got the nerves to ask me for money. Take it, Willy, make sure it lasts you a long time because it's the only thing you'll ever get from me, I promise you that." Willy never flinched as he eagerly picked up the money.

"Thanks, Dante. Thanks so much," he said smiling, displaying a front row of rotten teeth.

The scowl etched on Black's face was one of hurt, disappointment, pain, and resentment. Being pissed at his father for walking out on the family and being a drunk was one thing. But after seeing Yvonne, he realized that he had a lot of demons that he had to deal with. After gathering himself, Willy and his strung-out girlfriend headed across One Hundred and Tenth Street, to Miracles Liquor store. Black shook his head in disbelief as he stood there on the sidewalk watching both of them as they exited the liquor store and out of his sight.

***

Later that night . . .

"Hi, ma."

"Hi, Dante. How are you son?"

"I'm doing good, and you?"

"Well, everything is fine. Your aunt and I went to see Smokey Robinson last night at the Apollo."

"Oh, yeah! I forgot about it. How was it?"

"He was great, and he looks awfully good too," she said, laughing.

"So, you guys enjoyed yourselves?"

"We certainly did. So, what's going on with you?"

"I ran into dad earlier today."

"You did? Did you talk to each other?"

"Yeah, we spoke."

"How is he?"

"He's okay. He looks like he's still doing whatever it is he's doing."

"Still the same thing, huh? He needs some help," she sighed.

"I said the same thing. He knew about Joe-Joe and Lil Ray."

"So, what was his excuse for not showing up?"

"He said he wouldn't have been welcomed."

Shaking her head, his mother said, "I guess he'll probably do the same thing when the good Lord is ready for me."

"You ain't going nowhere ma, if anybody is going anywhere it's him." Shaking her head, Mrs. Reynolds had a troubled look on her face.

"Was that all?" she asked, realizing that Willy's absence affected Black more so than she had thought.

"I gave him some money."

"You did?"

"Yeah. At first, I didn't wanna give it to him because I know what he's gonna do with it."

"It's okay, son, God moves in mysterious ways."

"Yeah, he does ma, but I'll call you later. I have a few things to take care of."

"Okay, son, be careful."

"I will ma, later."

As Black drove on the Southern State Parkway, he couldn't forget the worried look on his mother's face, as he spoke about his father. He knew she still loved him, and this troubled him deeply.

***

Within minutes, he was back in Harlem. Once inside the safe house, he began telling Speedy about the encounter he had with his father.

"Ain't that some shit!" Speedy responded

"I couldn't believe that mutha-fucka. He looked like a bum. He was all fucked up. And hanging out with some toothless broke-down bitch, who told him she knew who I was. Not once did he ask about my mother or Adiba. The only thing he wanted was some cake. Drug money at that, go figure."

"You gave him that shit?"

"Yeah, I did."

"How much you gave him?"

"I don't know. I ain't count it. I gave him what I had in my pocket."

"Damn, Black! You hit him up good."

"Yeah, I know. I'm hoping that he drinks himself to death or shoots it up and o'd."

"He's using, too? Son, if your pops is using, that's fucked up."

"The crazy shit is, I don't know. I couldn't tell, but that bitch he was with, she looked like a fucking user."

"No doubt! I hear you."

"Speeds, it wouldn't surprise me if he's using. Damn!"

"Don't stress that, son. That's how shit is sometimes. Parents do dumb shit too, yo. They bring you into the world sometimes knowing they have problems, but instead of taking care of that shit before they bring a nigga into the world. They throw it up in your face so that you can see them fucking up. But a mutha-fucka don't wanna see their parents going through that shit, you feel me?"

"Yeah, you right, Speed, and what I saw in my mom's eyes tonight was real. I get it, son, death leaves a heartache no one can heal, and love leaves a memory no one can steal. I saw that tonight from my mom. I did."

"Damn, Black, that's some deep shit, son."

"Yeah," he said, seemingly in a daze.

For what it was worth, Speedy's words had a calming effect on him. They soon changed the topic of discussion to the business at hand. Black wanted to know how things turned out with Divine and his associates.

EPISODE 15

"What? How the fuck did this happen and when did this take place?" Black asked, angrily.

"It was that mutha-fucka, Tony Rome and his bitch, Winky. They rolled on Divine with like six other mutha-fuckas. They ate him and one of his contacts. The shit happened a few hours ago. They took everything. They lucky they ain't get merked. You know how that mutha-fucka Tony Rome be rolling," Speedy remarked.

"Hmm. So, they got my ten keys?" he said to no one in particular.

"Yeah, that and about thirty grand and an extra twelve keys."

"You fucking serious?"

"Hell, yeah!"

"How the fuck Divine let that happen? Where is he?"

"I think he's with his homies trying to figure out how they gonna get the shit back."

"Hit that nigga up and tell him to check me. Why you ain't hit me, Speeds?"

"I did, son. I called you mad times and all I got was your voice mail."

"Fuck! You right, damn! I had that shit off. Fuck me!" Black said, realizing he had turned his phone off minutes after he left his mother.

"I was wondering what was up when your voice mail came on."

"Let me ask you this? You think Divine set it?"

"Nah. The way shit went down; he couldn't have been down. Divine ain't got no love for Tony Rome. Plus, you know Tony Rome and his homies been doing a lot of grimey shit lately."

"Yeah, you right."

Although Divine wasn't an official member of the Syndicate, he was a childhood friend of theirs. Born Omar Gervin, he was a troubled youngster while growing up. He stood over six feet. He was dark in complexion with a squeaky voice that sounded like one of the many characters from the cartoon network. Like the rest of the crew, he felt that the drug game was his only way out of the ghetto. He had his crew. They controlled One Hundred and One, to One Hundred and Sixth Streets and First Avenue on the East side of Manhattan. He remained close with Black and Trigga and often did business with them.

"Yo, he just pulled up," Speedy hollered at Black, walking away from the window.

"Is he by himself?"

"Yeah!"

"Yo, Black, those niggas got me good," Divine said, entering the safe house.

"Yeah, I heard. What happened, yo?"

"Me and Infinite rolled up to Bradhurst and One Hundred and Thirty-Eight Street, where we met up with Charlie."

"Why, Charlie? What happened to that other cat? What's his name again?"

"You mean, Punch?" Speedy asked.

"Yeah, that's the mutha-fucka I'm talking about."

"He's outta town, so they send Charlie. Charlie is cool. I done copped shit from him mad times," Divine answered.

"True that. Go ahead."

"Yeah, son, me, Charlie and Infinite were waiting for the elevator at 465 Bradhurst. You know that fly ass building with the doorman security and all that shit right there on the corner?"

"Right!"

"When the elevator hit the first floor we got on. But there was a girl on it. She ain't get off though."

"That was that bitch!" Speedy asked.

"For real, son, she got off on the eighth floor. And we got off on the ninth. A dude was standing by a door fumbling with some keys. He was dressed like a mutha-fucking janitor. So, we ain't pay him no mind. We were about to enter the apartment when this punk pulled out on us with the bitch and some other cats who came out of nowhere.

They were all packing. Son, I couldn't even reach for my burner. They snatched the key from Charlie and took us inside. I thought they were gonna merk me, son. I was shitting bricks. I thought this was it. But all them punks wanted was the dough and the 'caine. We were lucky, yo. They took our jewelry and burners and left us tied up, naked. The shit was fucked up, Black."

"Word, y'all some lucky mutha-fuckas!"

“I know,” he stated, shaking his head.

“You know it’s that bitch ass, Tony Rome, Winky, and their homies who set y’all?” Black added.

“Yeah, son, we know. But who the fuck is Tony Rome?”

“That’s that wild ass mutha-fucka from One Hundred and Thirty-Sixth Street, he’s been hitting a lot of cats lately, him and that bitch, Winky,” Speedy remarked.

“So waddup with Charlie and them? What are they gonna do about it?” Black asked.

“Those niggas are ready to move on him. They know who he is. I heard of the brotha, but I’m like, who the fuck is he? He thinks he’s gonna run upon us, and take our shit and don’t do us? And think we ain’t gonna get him? That’s a dumb mutha- fucka, he must be dumbing out.”

“Check this out,” Black said, calmly. “We’re gonna take him and his bitch out. I wanna get them myself. Let’s do them before Charlie and his crew, you feel me? ‘Cause those cats might not wanna give us back our shit. And that will lead to some other shit. So, to avoid all the drama let’s take care of business first.”

“No doubt, Black,” Speedy snapped, as Divine nodded in agreement.

Days later . . .

Black, Speedy, Divine, and Infinite began casing Tony Rome’s neighborhood and the building where he did business. It wasn’t long before they spotted one of his workers entering the building.

“Don’t move mutha-fucka!” Black said, through clenched teeth, his weapon rubbing against the face of his intended victim.

"Don't shoot me, yo! I ain't moving, man! I ain't moving! Just don't shoot me!"

"Shut the fuck up, bitch!" Divine shouted, slamming his fist into his face. Terrified and pleading for his life, he was led to an apartment on the second floor.

"Who's inside?" Black asked in a commanding voice.

Shaking, he barely uttered, "Winky, Stokes, and some of the workers."

"Some? Give me numbers mutha-fucka!" he snapped, as he smacked him upside his head with his weapon.

"Three," he screamed. "You sure?"

"Yeah!"

"Where the fuck is Tony Rome?" Divine asked.

"I don't know, but he should be back in a minute."

"Here's what you're gonna do. You're gonna knock on the door and be cool about it, you feel me?" Black said.

"A'aight, son. You got it," he stammered.

"Who the fuck is it?" a male voice asked from behind the door.

"It's me, open the door, Stokes." There was a loud boom as the men shoved their way inside the apartment, quickly overpowering Stokes and the others.

"Be cool mutha-fuckas, be cool!" Black yelled.

Knowing that she was in a life-and-death situation, Winky reached for her weapon. Three slugs tore into her body throwing her against the widescreen television in the living room.

"I'm cool! I'm cool!" Stokes pleaded.

"Tie them niggas up. Y'all get on the mutha- fucking floor," Black snapped.

With only the white of their eyes showing and their mouths wide open and fearing for their lives, they were pleading and crying like babies. Winky was still breathing when Divine walked over to her and asked, "Where's our shit?"

"What shit?" she asked, through blood-clenched teeth.

"Bitch! You don't remember me, huh? Act like you don't know, but I got something for your ass."

With his gun cocked, Divine stared in her eyes and said, "Wink, bitch!" and fired a round into her forehead. Stokes and the others shitted on themselves as their eyes filled with terror and shifted from side to side.

"These mutha-fuckas stinks! Take them in the back!" Black said. "And chill and wait for that pussy, Rome!"

"Oh, shit! Yo, check this out!" Infinite yelled, pulling a half-full Glad trash bag filled with cash and cocaine.

"Anything else in here?" Black asked.

"No, no, that's it," the men responded.

"Search this bitch," Divine said.

They were waiting patiently while contemplating whether to wait out Rome or just take the stash they found. But their prayers were answered. There was a knock on the door. Black quietly peered through the peephole. Seeing it was Tony Rome, he opened the door as the others snatched him inside the apartment before he could reach for his weapon.

"Hey, yo! What the fuck is up? What's all this, y'all?" Tony Rome screamed.

"You fucked with the wrong mutha-fuckas!" Speedy snarled as Black stuck his weapon in his nostril.

"Black, I didn't know it was your shit! Son, I didn't know! You know I wouldn't have fucked with your shit. The shit is here, you can have it back. I'm sorry, yo! I'm begging you. I swear I didn't know. Speedy, you know me, yo! Tell him, yo! It ain't got to go down like this!" Tony Rome begged, deliberately avoiding Divine's eyes.

"It's a little too late for that," Black growled.

"I only took the shit. I ain't hurt nobody. Come on, Black! You ain't got to do me like that!"

"Fuck that nigga, Black!" an irate Divine said.

Without saying another word, they opened fire on the men. Their bodies were hit repeatedly. They made sure that no one made it out alive. As they inspected the bodies, they fired an additional round in their forehead before snatching up the Glad garbage bag and leaving the apartment.

***

After their ensuing takedown of Tony Rome and Winky, the men remained low-key, while conducting their business. Charlie and his crew heard about the hit. However, they couldn't say whether it was the Syndicate, Divine, or someone else who pulled it off. When the hit took place, Rome was a wanted man, so it could have been any of his many enemies. His demise was inevitable.

Black was more than pleased, as he, Infinite, Speedy, and Divine split the cash and cocaine. They also continued to do business with Charlie and his people. It was during this period that he met Infinite's younger sister, Tricia Simpson, also called Bird. Despite Infinite's disapproval of her joining his crew, she paid him no mind. An obsessed neurotic, possessive, calculating, vivacious, and attractive young woman, she was respected by the neighborhood thugs because of her boyish ways growing up; and later her involvement as a low-budget drug dealer.

Her reputation was solid, and so was her .40 Glock. She was one of the most feared members of her brother and Divine's crew. She wouldn't hesitate to take a life if it meant saving her own. Honey brown in complexion, she was an athletic five-foot-nine with a gorgeous figure. She was well-toned, and in great shape with a ridiculous six-pack. The two years she spent at the Women's House on Rikers Island had toughened her up.

Black was charmed by her beauty, physique, and candid disposition; he loved that about her. At the age of sixteen, she shot her boyfriend of two years, because he mistreated her during her pregnancy. She was later arrested and faced several years in jail. She took a plea and ended up doing two years of a one and a half to three-year sentence. She was always supportive of her brother and fought many of his battles when they were kids. Being the oldest, she was more or less his protector. Despite the support that he got from his sister; Infinite never backed down from a fight.

Those closest to Black knew he was smitten by Bird's beauty and kept Maria away. Maria saw Bird on a few occasions but thought nothing of it. If anything, she thought she was seeing Speedy or one of the other crew members. Although Bird was an unofficial member of the Syndicate, it never stopped her from hanging out with the crew. And Black certainly made it his business to have her around.

***

Always fearing the worst, Black wasn't surprised upon hearing that Charlie and his crew knew he was responsible for taking down Tony Rome. Charlie made it known that he wanted his product returned. Black smiled as the story was relayed to him. Just then the phone rang, it was Trigga.

"What's up with that, Black?" Speedy asked with a screw face.

"Gimme a minute!" He continued talking on the phone with Trigga. "Tell you what, let me call you back. Matter of fact, why don't you come check me?" Hanging up the phone, he turned to Speedy and said, "It doesn't matter what that mutha- fucka says. What matters is that we got his shit and we keeping the mutha-fucka. Do you feel me on this, son? It's all lip service. We'll deal with it."

Inside the stash house were Black, Speedy, Divine, Infinite, Bird, Fats, and Bee along with several of their workers. The men were still talking when Trigga arrived.

"Yo, Charlie and them ain't no joke. We can't be fucking with them niggas and take them lightly. Those some serious mutha-fuckas, so we have to be just as vicious," Divine emphasized.

"Don't worry about Charlie; he's a minor player in this. The cats we have to worry about are Punch, Coolio, and their boss, Hits. They the mutha- fuckas we have to take out first. And then everything else will run cool, you hear me, rude boy?" Trigga said staring at Black.

"That shit makes sense," Black agreed.

"I never liked those mutha-fuckas anyway," Bird retorted. "I don't know why Divine started fucking with them in the first place."

"The bottom line is this. How are we gonna take them? Are we gonna do them one at a time or do them all at the same time?" Black asked, wanting to hear how they felt.

"It doesn't matter," Fats replied.

"It does matter!" he warned.

"That fat ass mutha-fucka Punch always eats at Hirachi, a Japanese restaurant in the city. He's usually with two or three bodyguards. He's easy bait," Infinite added.

"I don't give a fuck how many bodyguards he's got with him," Bird said aloud.

"Word!" Infinite agreed.

"I'll take all those bitches out by myself. I don't give a fuck!" she snapped, gripping the handle of her Glock.

"Bomboclatt, Black, she sounds like a terrorist!" The room fell out in laughter.

"Yeah, son! She be o'd'ing," Black said. Listen up y'all! This is how it's going down. Bird, Speedy, and Divine, y'all take care of Punch. This weekend, we'll take care of Coolio and Hits. Fats and Bee will do the driving," Black ended.

EPISODE 16

"Do you wanna go shopping with me?" Maria asked, Mercedes.

"Yeah, if you buy me some gears."

"Duh! What do you think? I got you, don't worry about it."

"Where are you going?"

"The Prada and Gucci store."

"Oh, shit, my cousin is going hard."

Hopping into Maria's SUV, the women who hadn't seen each other in a while had a lot of catching up to do as they drove to Manhattan. Their first stop was the Prada store, and as Maria browsed through the aisles, she felt a tap on her shoulder.

"How are you doing, Maria?" a male voice asked.

"Hey," she responded, startled for a second, before recognizing who it was. "You came shopping by yourself? Where are your friends at?"

"They back at the spot. But I always do my shopping by myself."

"That's mad cool. So, what's up? Oh, this is my cousin."

"Nice meeting you," he replied.

"Nice meeting you too," she answered. He couldn't keep his eyes off Maria as she continued shopping.

"Can I have a word with you?" he asked, interrupting her and Mercedes' conversation.

"About what?"

"It's some personal shit, it's really important."

"Sure," she responded, stepping aside, curious to find out what was so important and personal.

"When can we talk?"

"I'll let you know."

"Why don't you give me your number?"

"You know I can't do that; Dante would kill me."

"A'ight, take mine instead."

"I can't do that either. Whatever it is that you have to tell me, we can meet up somewhere."

"Name the place."

"I'll be at Manhattan Center tomorrow at 2:00 p.m., meet me there."

"A'ight, I'll be there, one."

"What's up with that dude?" Mercedes asked.

"He said he's got something important to tell me," Maria answered.

"I don't trust him. He was checking you out the whole time. He was acting like he wanted to fuck you."

"You think I didn't see it? I saw that shit. Dante would do him if he tried anything stupid. I just wanna know what he's got to say."

"He works for Black?"

"Yeah! That's what I'm telling you, he wouldn't play himself like that."

"I don't care what you say. He was checking you out."

"You're taking this shit way too seriously. You need to stop."

"No, I'm not," she said, laughing. "It's just that . . ."

"Just what? He's cute, right? Come on, don't lie!"

"Yeah, he's cute, but he doesn't look like he can be trusted."

"I'll let you know what's going down after I get the info." The women completed their shopping and then headed home. Maria kept her word as promised.

When Black got home that night, Maria's behavior disturbed him. She would ask certain questions and instead of waiting for a response; she would smile and change the topic. This irritated him. Seeing that she wouldn't share whatever it was that was on her mind, he took a shower and went to bed.

***

The next day . . .

"I bet you thought I wasn't gonna show up, huh?" the brother said, with a smile on his face.

"Nah, I knew you would," Maria replied. "Well, what is so important that you have to tell me?"

He was pacing back and forth with an unsure look on his face before finally saying, "It's your man, he's fucking with Bird." Maria stood there silently as the words hit her like a Roger Clemens fastball.

"Hold the fuck up! You're telling me that Dante is fucking, Bird?"

"Yeah, I'm telling you that!"

"How do you know this?"

"Maria, be real, you talking to me."

"And why are you telling me this?" she questioned him.

"I just think what he's doing to you is fucked up. And you don't deserve any of that bullshit."

"Is that so, and what's in it for you? It must be something?"

"Ain't nothin' in it for me, that's on the real!"

"What I wanna know is what did he do to you? He had to do something?"

"He ain't do nothin' to me."

"And you expect me to believe this?"

"Nah, I want you to know this."

"And what if I do? Where's the proof?"

"I got proof, don't worry."

"Ain't you and Dante like really tight? You guys have been tight for a minute, right?"

"Yeah, but what that got to do with what I'm telling you? He's doing you grimey. He doing that shit in everybody's face and nobody wants to say anything about it. I just feel you deserve better."

"You do, huh?"

"You know what? I'll even make sure I have pictures of them the next time I see you. There will be a next time, right?"

"Sure, three days from today."

"Where? Here?"

"Yeah, here is cool!" Maria had an intense look on her face as she studied his, before walking away.

***

The three days couldn't come any sooner, as Maria anticipated what other surprises would be next. "Here are the pictures I promised you," the brother said with a slight smile on his face. Maria was calm as she stared at the photographs. She was aware of Black's infidelities, but to see him in action pissed her off. She wanted to keep the photos as proof to show him. However, he refused to hand them over to her. Maria thanked him and began walking towards her car. Her mind was racing back and forth. She was angry. Her emotions were at the boiling point.

She never confronted Black about the photographs. Whenever they argued about his infidelities, she never mentioned Bird by name. She would lump all his women in one basket and curse him about them. She loved him dearly, and despite his cheating ways, he loved her. He told his lovers that she was off-limits, and he wasn't going to leave her, and they either had to deal with it or move on.

***

Maria finally builds up her nerves and asked Black about his infidelities. He was his usual playful self.

"Why is that bitch always around you, Dante?"

"Who are you talking about?"

"I'm talking about that bitch, Bird!"

"Bird? Come on now, Maria! She's the one giving us the info on that bitch, Melissa."

"Okay, Dante. I'm stupid!"

"Bird isn't always around me. She's around everybody. Why you always gotta come at me like that? Every woman that comes around the crew you have a problem with, why is that?"

"You a fucking liar, Dante! I only have a problem with the bitches you stick your dick in. You know what the fuck I'm talking about. Don't act like you don't know."

"I don't know what you talking about. You reading too much into this nonsense, ain't nothin' happening."

He thought about mentioning the conversation that he and Mercedes had, which she knew nothing about; and her behavior over the past few days, where she would be gone for hours but decided against it.

"Keep thinking I'm stupid, Dante. You keep thinking that. You try and play me, a'ight? You just try it and see what happens!"

"Maria, stop it, baby! It ain't like that. I love you, and you've nothin' to worry about."

After calming her down, he assured her that there wasn't anything going on between him and Bird, and if anything did happen; she was just a fuck, and he didn't want her. He said this to calm her down hoping that she would tell him her little secret, but she didn't fall for it.

Instead, she smiled, and said she understood. If he wanted to play games she would play right along, and he felt the same. He then took a shower, got dressed, and headed to the safe house. There, he met up with Bird and the others. Taking Bird aside, he whispered in her ear as the others pretended as if they didn't see a thing.

"We'll see you guys later," Black said, as they headed out the door. Minutes later, they arrived at Bird's, Queens Village apartment.

EPISODE 17

The Syndicate was mired in several gang wars. The stench of death reeked continuously around them, and as they concluded that the time was right to carry out the hit on Punch, they would see firsthand, Bird's psychopathic and abnormal behavior up close. Black gave them the green light, and the crew responded.

"Do you see their whips?" Divine asked as they exited the car.

"Yeah," Bird answered.

"Y'all wanna wait for them out here, or y'all wanna walk up in there and do 'em? Yo, say something!" Speedy said, waiting for a response.

"What do you think, Bird?" Divine asked.

"Fuck this! I'm going in that bitch!" she said, putting on the mask she brought with her. With their masks on, and following closely behind, Bird entered the restaurant with two.40 Glocks in her hands blazing.

"Oh, my God!" Several patrons screamed.

The sounds echoed inside the restaurant as Bird, Speedy, and Divine opened fire. Hit in the face and torso, Punch never had a chance. His two bodyguards were also cut down in a hail of bullets. As several patrons hid under the tables, they walked over to the bullet-riddled bodies of the men and fired a round in each of their foreheads.

"They executed them!" someone yelled.

"Who were they? Did anyone see their faces?" a gentleman in a business suit asked.

"One of them looked like a girl!" a fat man shouted as he used his body as a shield to protect his wife and young daughter.

"Call the cops! Call the cops!" a cook yelled.

"Fuck this! I'm getting the fuck outta here!" a young man who happened to be walking past the restaurant with his friends said.

With Bee behind the wheels, the Black Escalade sped off with its tires screeching.

"We got the mutha-fuckas!" Bird said, gleefully.

"For a second there I thought you were me, Bird!" Speedy exclaimed, excitedly.

"What do you mean?"

"Cause' that's some shit I would have said."

"Word!" she said, as they laughed. Bird reached into her pocket and pulled out a small notebook. She wrote something down and then put a checkmark next to it.

"What's up with that?" Speedy asked as Divine looked on.

"This? Oh, this is nothin'," she replied as they drove towards the West Side Highway.

Once they were back in the stash house, Divine mentioned Bird's odd behavior to Black. They both agreed that something was wrong with her. Despite her outlandish behavior at times, Black loved her.

The next day . . .

Coolio and Hits demanded to know who carried out the hit, as they questioned several of their goons. They were dumbfounded, as their questions and searches led to nowhere. Yet they continued with the threats hoping someone would provide some information.

"Let them mutha-fuckas keep guessing! Those cats are just like Tony Rome and his crew. They have been getting death threats since day one. All we got to do is just chill and then hit them again," Black reassured them.

"These mutha-fuckas are crazy, Black! They sending us threats like we pussies or something. What's up with that?" Speedy retorted.

"I guess they wanted their shit, but fuck that! Look, how many mutha-fuckas owed them? A lot, right? And all we had for them bitches were a few kilos. Fuck them!"

"That's what's up," Bird agreed.

"Hey, Black, we can't afford to let up now. We gotta put the heat on them mutha-fuckas. Right now, our crews have to be ready twenty-four seven. We have to be ready to answer any pussy who thinks they can disrespect," Trigga warned them.

"No doubt."

Everyone had left except for Speedy, Black, and Peanut when Speedy asked Black why he didn't bring Riff on any of the hits.

"It ain't like that Speedy, remember Suzy is locked down. Me and you are busy with these mutha fuckas so why not let Riff handle some of the business, you feel me? I don't want them old ass niggas like Fats and Bee running our shit."

"No doubt, that's what's up, huh?"

"That's what I'm talking about, give him some experience," he said, laughing. "Yo, Im'a about to make this move, you wanna roll?"

"A'ight."

"Yo, Peanut, when Riff gets here, tell him to meet us in Crown Heights. I don't know why that nigga ain't got his phone on," Black said, walking out the door.

"Cool," Peanut answered.

***

Black was driving at a moderate speed on the FDR Drive. He couldn't help himself as he thought about Ray and Joe. He felt guilty and blamed himself because he had been powerless to protect either of them. The name and whereabouts of Ray's killer were still unknown to him. Yet he was confident that Speedy would find out who the culprits were. As he sped toward the Brooklyn Bridge, he drifted off once again. *So much is going on; I don't know what's up anymore,* he said to himself, as Suzy came to mind.

The lawyers he hired were doing their best; still, it wasn't enough for him. *This shit is a mutha- fucka!* He mumbled, taking a glance at Speedy, who had fallen asleep.

He had a lot on his mind, and the thing that kept him sane was knowing that Adiba was doing well in law school. He was happy for her because unlike him, she was making their mother proud. He knew he could have probably done something other than getting into the drug game, which would have made her proud, like keeping his ass in school, but he chose this life and he now had to deal with it.

As lightning flashed across the sky, and the roaring thunder echoed loudly, Mother Nature's rain-soaked the streets and slowed traffic to a halt. Preoccupied with the issues confronting him, Black drove at a fast pace. Suddenly, the car began skidding on the sleek wet street.

"Are you okay?" Speedy asked, snapping out of his sleep.

"Yeah," he smiled.

"I was just thinking about a few things."

"A'ight, don't think too much though," he laughed.

Black pulled up in front of Coleman Inc. on Court Street and headed to the office of his business partner, who immediately sensed something wrong. Though he tried to downplay the whole thing, his business partner saw the troubled look on his face.

"Hey, you look a bit worried, what's been going on?"

"Man! I've been thinking about getting out of the business once my sister finishes law school," Black said, taking a seat.

"Really?"

"Yeah, I need someone who's gonna have my back at all times, and there is no better support than family, and for me to have her full support, I can't be doing this shit!"

"This is something that I never expected to hear in a million years. But I can understand what you are trying to do with all the legitimate businesses you are now operating."

"What else can I say? It's gonna be an awfully hard decision."

"Yes, it will."

"I'm making a lot of money, but I'm getting tired. My wife wants me to leave the game. She thinks I'm fucking every bitch that looks my way. All this shit, man . . . it's like what the fuck do I do? Where the fuck do I turn, you feel me?"

Speedy had a puzzled look on his face as he spoke. Black had never spoken to him about quitting the business, nor did he ever give the impression that he felt that way. After going over the necessary paperwork with Black, his business partner advised him not to make any rash decision based solely on emotions. Nodding, Black shook his hand and headed out the door. As soon as they got in the car, Speedy asked him if he was serious about giving up the business.

"I might because I'm getting tired of all the killings. First, it was Daryl, Crip, Joe-Joe, and now, Ray. Mutha-fuckas getting killed down south and in the Midwest, that's too much damn killing, son. Then Maria found out that me and Bird are fucking. My sources told me that someone in the crew got a hold of some pictures of me and Bird together."

"Son, are you serious? Yo, we got to find out who did that shit and merk that mutha-fucka. Whoever did that shit violated big time, son!"

"Don't worry son, we'll deal with it, a'ight?"

"Just say the word, son. I'll take care of it."

"I know, but still, all this drama is too much. Then a nigga gotta be on the lookout for some of these grimey dick-sucking bitches. These ho's will set a brotha up in a minute. Then I have to deal with these fucked up corrupt cops who don't give a fuck about any of us."

"No doubt, Black! That mutha-fucka Woody and his partners are the real mutha-fuckas we need to be clocking. I hate the fucking po-po! I ain't got no love for lawyers, court officers, judges, courthouses, stenographers, the courtrooms, or the fucking system. I hate all that shit! It shouldn't be our niggas dropping out. It should be Woody and all those mutha-fuckas," Speedy said, excitedly.

"The game is changing. Mutha-fuckas are getting hyped for the dumbest reasons including the po-po. And on the other hand, I have to deal with Maria and my family. This shit is getting hectic, yo. It's a lot, but I'm not ready to quit just yet, even though I'm thinking about it, you feel me? But we still have some unfinished business to take care of. We can't sleep on cats like Charlie and them. The minute they sneeze, we gotta do them."

"Yeah. I feel you. I ain't going nowhere, yo! Damn! Maria wants you to give up the game too?"

"You feel me?"

"I guess you spoiled her, Black."

"Maybe I did," he said, laughing.

"Cool. I can understand Maria and your fam, but them other niggas? Fuck them! This is it for me, Black. Fuck them mutha-fuckas! Fuck the world! Those mutha-fuckas ain't never give a fuck about us, son. We had to get our own and do our shit. Fuck them bitches!" Black was laughing as Speedy kept ranting.

"Shit! We was supposed to meet Riff in Crown Heights. Hit that nigga for me. If his voice mail comes on, just hang up."

"No doubt! I got his voice mail."

"Cool. You're right, Speedy, nobody gave us a damn thing. Half those big shot mutha-fuckas never came to our hoods offering us any jobs. And even when we looked downtown, they always dissed us. And like the Notorious B.I.G. use to say, 'No wonder Christmas missed us.' They don't know our situation. They don't know the problems we experienced here in the hood. You right, Speed. Fuck them all! But let me ask you this?"

"Go ahead, son."

"I know I've said it many times too, but what you think about mutha-fuckas not snitching when shit goes down?"

"That's the code son, those are the rules."

"I know, but the shit that we do is different. We chose this life, you feel me?"

"What you saying, Black?"

"I'm saying that the shit that happened last week in Brooklyn, where that twelve-year-old kid got merked in front of the White Castle and a bunch of mutha-fuckas was out there, and no one said anything to the po-po. That's the shit I'm talking about. That shit is different from our shit, you know. What about that little boy's mom, his family, you know, his friends?"

"Son, I don't know, that's some shit right there, it is. But I ain't know you was looking at shit like that."

"It's all this shit that's been happening. Plus, I got my little one, what if some shit were to happen to her? You see where I'm going with this?"

"I feel you, son. That's a hard one right there."

"Look how we grew up? We learned about the saggy pants, the du-rags, and keeping it real by not snitching from those cats in jail. That shit got me thinking, especially since I plan on having more kids. It does man, it does!"

"Yo, Black, you got me fucked up, son. I don't know what to say! I hear you, but I don't know!"

"It was just a thought, don't worry about it."

EPISODE 18

"Docket number 009456, Vincent Martinez!" a bailiff barked in a clear voice.

"Good morning your honor," the prosecutor said.

Suzy's jailhouse swagger was evident as he strolled into the courtroom smiling. He glanced at the judge and nodded at his aunts, Maria, Mercedes, and several of his friends.

"Your honor, Mr. Martinez was arrested on the 6th of June 2004. He was arrested at the corner of Crotona and Tremont Avenues in the Crotona section of the Bronx, less than three blocks from where three vicious and malicious murders were committed. Mr. Martinez was wounded in the left leg while engaged in a shootout at the Belmont Avenue location, where the murders were committed.

Mr. Martinez, your honor, was only thirty feet away from a nine-millimeter Glock handgun when he was apprehended. Your honor, given Mr. Martinez's extensive criminal background and record and the seriousness of this crime, I ask that the defendant be denied bail. Thank you, your honor!"

"Thank you, counsel," the judge replied. Suzy had a worried look on his face as the judge motioned for his lawyer to speak.

"Good morning your honor," his lawyer said. "Your honor, although when my client was arrested, he was wounded and a gun was found thirty feet from where he was apprehended, does not mean my client committed any wrongdoing or is he a murderer. My client was not the perpetrator of any crime. Furthermore, I contend that my client was shot in the leg while fleeing a gun battle between rival drug gangs, which he had nothing to do with. Moreover, the weapon that was found was either dropped or placed there by the actual perpetrators who were fleeing the scene. In no way or form did my client have anything to do with this incident. He was just an innocent bystander. Therefore, your honor, I ask that the court take into consideration that even though my client has been arrested in the past, he was a juvenile at the time, and he was never convicted of any crime. Thus, I ask that your honor, grant Mr. Martinez bail."

Suzy's heart was pounding as the Judge moved rather uneasily in his chair as he stared at him. Looking over the documents in front of him, he set bail of $1.5 million. Suzy had a slight smile on his face as he whispered a few words in his lawyer's ear. He waved, smiled, and gave the thumbs-up sign to his family and friends. He still had his swagger as he was escorted to the holding pen for the ride back to Rikers Island. His lawyer approached the family and relayed his message. The family was delighted he was given bail. Black was happy for Maria. She was teary-eyed as she told him how things turned out.

***

The same couldn't be said about Melissa, who had gone into hiding months earlier. Her luck had run out, and for what it was worth, she would come face to face with Black and the Syndicate.

"Yo, Black, we found out where that bitch, Melissa lives!" Speedy informed him.

"So, what are you waiting on?"

"We on it."

It was a cool night, as Melissa and her friends clowned each other as they sipped and smoked "L's". Melissa, who lived at One Hundred and Sixty-Ninth Street and College Avenue in the Bronx, wasn't far from her home when she decided to walk to the Kennedy Fried Chicken, a few blocks from where she lived.

"Daag, y'all ain't coming?" she asked her friends.

"Yeah. As soon as we finish this shit," they said.

"Fuck that! I got the munchies!" she said, upset that they wanted her to wait.

"Yo, bring us some of that shit you getting," a male friend of hers said, as he began rolling another marijuana blunt.

"Fuck y'all! I ain't bringing y'all shit! Psych!"

"Yo, here!" the dude rolling the blunt said, as he handed her a twenty-dollar bill.

"I'll be right back." She never saw the car following her, nor did her friends. Riff and Bee quickly approached her with their guns drawn and shoved her into the car.

"What the fuck!" a frightened Melissa yelled, her eyes darting back and forth at the men.

"Hi!" Speedy smiled.

"Who the fuck is you?" Melissa asked, not knowing who the men were.

"Oh! This bitch got jokes, son! This bitch stared me down like a real thug, yo. And she wants to know who the fuck we are? Update her," Speedy laughed with wild eyes.

"Bitch! We are Ray's homies! That's who we are!" Riff snapped, as the car sped across the Grand Concourse toward Jerome Avenue. Melissa's high quickly hit a downward spiral and gradually disappeared.

"It wasn't me!" she began sobbing. "I had nothin' to do with it!"

"So, who was it then?" Riff said aloud.

"Leave it alone Riff, when we get to Harlem, she'll tell us everything. Ain't that right, Melissa?" Black said with a cold stare.

Seeing the scowl on Black's face, and the continuous stares from the others, she immediately felt the urge to release her bladder. She tried desperately to hold her pee, but it was all in vain, as she pissed all over herself. They brazenly took her from the car and whisked her inside an old brownstone that they used for important business. Waiting inside the apartment were Bird and Divine.

"So, this is the bitch?" Black asked aloud.

"The one and only," Speedy sinisterly replied.

"What do you know about my cousin's death?" he asked. With her head held low and her eyes staring at the floor, she didn't respond.

"Bitch, you heard what he said!" Bird snapped, slapping her across the face with a crushing backhand. "Who the fuck did it?"

"It was Tyesha, she set it up with a guy name Shrug from Webster Avenue," she bellowed.

"Where on Webster?" Black asked.

"He is around the Butler Houses." Fearing the worst, she began to cry.

"Hmm, so what happened? What went down?" he asked, telling her to take a seat.

"We knew he was coming to the party with Trina. So, Shrug paid me and Tyesha to get him in the room. But I only wanted to have sex with him. I didn't know he was gonna shoot him. Tyesha was the one who set everything up. She's friends with them. I only got in it because of the money I was promised. I swear. I didn't know they were gonna do that to him."

"Where does Tyesha live?" Black demanded.

"Valentine Avenue and One Hundred and Eighty-First Street."

"Bitch! What's the number, and what does she look like? Do you have a telephone number for her?"

"Yeah," Melissa whimpered, scared, and terrified.

"Call her and tell her that you and your cousin are coming by."

Melissa did as she was told, and within minutes, Tyesha was in the car with her and Speedy, as they headed to the "death gates". The others followed closely behind.

"Get the fuck off me! What the fuck is y'all doing?" Tyesha yelled once they were inside. Wham! She was reeling backward after Bird smacked her across the face and told her to shut up.

"Melissa says you were the one who set up Ray! Is that true?" Black asked.

"That bitch is lying! It wasn't me! She lying!"

"So, you both are telling the truth?"

"It was Shrug!" she cried.

"Hmm! Let me get this right, Shrug paid both of you to set up, Ray? But y'all didn't know he was gonna kill him? Y'all thought it was only gonna be a beat down? Is that right?"

"Yeah," she stammered.

"She's lying. She knew they were gonna kill him! She the one who was with them when they shot that other dude, Crip," Melissa screamed.

"What the fuck! This is her? This bitch is a killer, huh, fellas? So, this is the bitch that shot Crip and set up my cousin?" Black said, turning toward the others. "I understand. I get it. Yeah, I get it."

The men looked at each other. There wasn't a lot left to be said. They were watching Black's every move as he nodded at Speedy before walking away.

"Please don't! Oh, my God! No, no, no!" the two girls wailed.

Bird and Bee put their weapons to Melissa's head and fired. Her head jerked and then fell limp as she hit the floor. Tyesha began screaming in anguish. Her yells were eerie as they echoed throughout the second floor.

"Shut the fuck up!" Riff shouted as he opened fire hitting her twice in the mouth. Blood flowed from her mouth as she fell on her back. Barely alive, she stared into the eyes of Riff, who froze momentarily after seeing the look on her face. As she choked on her blood, Bird snatched the gun from his hand and fired several rounds at point-blank range into her forehead.

When the shooting stopped, Black quietly observed the carnage. He had a pleased look on his face as he ordered the men to remove the bodies, "Y'all know what to do get rid of everything and remember no mistakes."

"It's all good, we'll take care of it," Speedy replied.

Bird then pulled out her black book without anyone noticing and wrote in it. The next day, Black received news of Peanut's death. Peanut was recently promoted and was moving up in the hierarchy of the organization when he was gunned down by several of Tony Rome's goons in Spanish Harlem. He was killed over a drug deal that went sour when the men he was doing business with recognized him.

EPISODE 19

It was a Saturday night, and Black was chilling at the safe house with the crew. They were sipping on Hennessy and smoking "L's". Caught up in all the hoopla, he didn't realize how late it was. Seeing that he was in no condition to drive, he called Maria and told her he would be home late. He quickly fell asleep with Bird next to him.

"Oh, shit!" he said to no one in particular when he woke up, "I've got to get my ass home."

Maria was furious. She was frustrated, angry, and hurt. She felt she was losing him, and that he was doing nothing to prevent it. She was making breakfast when he walked into the kitchen. Without saying a word, she flung the coffee machine at him. It crashed against the wall barely missing his head.

"What's wrong with you?" he said, with a serious look on his face.

"What the fuck you mean, what's wrong with me? Where were you last night?"

"Come on now! I've been out before!"

"Yes, you have, but you called!"

He didn't know what to say. The only thing he could come up with was, "I was hanging with the fellas, and lost track of time. And I did call."

"Look at the time you called? You could have been considerate and called much earlier. You don't give a damn about either me or our child! I'm beginning to get the impression that you don't care. Because if you did, you wouldn't treat us the way you do. When was the last time you took your daughter to the park? When was the last time you played a game with either of us? Or give us a hug or a kiss? When Dante? When, mutha-fucka? All you do is come in late and say you are tired and then you wanna fuck. Is that it, Dante? You just wanna fuck? Baby, I'm tired of this shit, isn't there something that you need to tell me? When are you gonna come clean, huh? When? Why are you forcing my hands? Why are you doing this to me, when will it stop?"

"I didn't know you were taking shit like this. I ain't got nothin' to come clean about! What am I supposed to come clean about? Tell me?"

"Oh, fuck! I can't believe you, Dante! I can't believe you!"

"I know I have been messing up, but damn!" he said, hoping she would come clean also.

"Damn, what?"

"I thought you would understand," he stuttered, speechless.

"What should I understand?"

"Listen, babes, I'm stressed. I've been stressed from all the bullshit that's been going on. I'm worried about your cousin's situation. Plus, I have to come up with the money to bail him out. Then niggas are dying left and right. Even my cousin and people that were close to me are dead.

Mutha-fuckas are coming up short on the product. The police are tearing up my spots, and I've been thinking about everything you said about walking away from the game. What the hell do you want me to do, Maria? How am I supposed to cope?"

"Quit, Dante, that's how you cope. Give up the damn illegal part of the business!"

"That's easier said than done. Come on now, babes! I told you it's not that easy. I just can't give up the business like that. What about the dirt you have done, don't look at me like you're shocked?"

"What about me, Dante?"

"You were the one who set that mutha-fucka, Choco."

"Don't even go there. Don't even try that! But you know what? Okay, I did that to Choco, you're right! I did my shit! I did my dirt! But I'm tired of that life. Is that a crime? It's the shit you do that made me do the shit I did."

"I did, huh? And what was it that I drove you to do?" he exclaimed, hoping she would come clean about the pictures she had of him and Bird. Instead, what she was about to say was something he would have never imagined.

"I thought about cheating on you. Yes, I did!"

"What? With who?"

"One of your close friends, I was gonna do it to get back at you and Bird."

"You were gonna cheat on me with one of my friends to get back at me and Bird? Is that right?" He was outraged, and he pointed a shaking finger at her. He was trying his best to control his anger as he began ranting and swearing. Despite his angry outburst, she stood her ground.

"You did this to me. You know I love you. I love my child. I'm your wife. I care about you, and I want to grow old with you. I want to have more children, Dante. Whenever you leave the house, I get scared. Every time the telephone rings, I jump. I get scared thinking that you are in jail or worse, dead. Tell me; am I wrong for being concerned?"

She was crying as she sat down at the kitchen table and told him that she saw the pictures of him and Bird, but she later got rid of them. She tried to compose herself. Getting up, she walked into the living room. Even as a little girl, she wanted to get married and have a family. That was the dream of most young girls, and now that she was married, she wanted to make it work.

Although Black was pissed at her, he knew he was to blame. He knew she was right, and for the first time in his life, he was speechless. He apologized. He reached out to her and held her gently in his arms as he consoled her and tried to reassure her everything would be fine. He knew he had to do something. Then it suddenly hit him, he called Speedy and told him, he was in charge of the operation for the next two weeks.

He then told Maria to make reservations for two to Atlantic City. With the problems of the drug world, Bird, and other concerns now temporarily behind him, he had more than enough time to reflect on his family.

***

While he was enjoying his two-week vacation, the police department launched "Operation Hierarchy." Its primary goal was to arrest the head of the drug gangs in the city. Using the low-level street dealers as baits and pressuring them, many became informants, fearing entrapment.

Woody and his goons also made their intentions known. They demanded a bigger share of the money and drugs and asked the organization to limit some of its activities. He and his goons were pissed when Speedy told them no.

"Do you know who you're fucking with?" he shouted, banging his fist against the door.

"No doubt!" Speedy replied, nonchalant. "But you need to save all this lip service for Black."

"If Black is not at the next meeting, then our deal is off!" he angrily shouted, before storming out the room.

"I'll tell him what you said," Speedy responded with his trademark sinister smile.

Black was somewhat apprehensive when informed about these new developments. He knew they needed the protection, and upon his return from Atlantic City, he went ahead and made the necessary changes.

EPISODE 20

One month later . . .

"Damn! This smells good!" Suzy said, as he inhaled the cool New York air and screamed, "I'm free!" Hopping into Maria's Mercedes Benz, he couldn't help himself as he reclined his seat and smiled. "It feels good to be back out in the world!"

"I can tell," she said smiling, happy that he was home.

"Yeah, it's good to be home. I missed y'all big time!"

"We missed you too, Suzy, especially me."

"Thanks, cuz, but I need a forty and a few L's right about now."

"No, Cristal?"

"Nah, cuz! I need some piss juice. Some real live hood shit," he declared, staring at the asses of several girls as they drove by.

"You're crazy!" Maria said, laughing.

"I'm gonna drop by Rosie's crib and hit that pussy."

"Damn! I don't wanna hear all that. You've got it all figured out, huh?"

"That's what's up, cuz, that's how it be, you feel me?"

"I hear you. They're waiting inside to see you," Maria said to him, pulling into the driveway.

"I'm glad you home, son!" Black said as he greeted him.

"Thanks, Black. Thanks for getting me out," a grateful Suzy said.

"Don't worry about it. You would have done the same for me."

"True that!" he retorted, extending his hand. "Come on now, give me a fucking hug!"

Black smiled, putting his arms around him. As they embraced, he said, "I want you to stay away from the game and keep a low profile. Maria will hit you with whatever you need, you feel me? Just chill, a'ight?"

"I got you, Black. I'll do that."

"Cool. I'll hit you later, okay," Black said, telling Maria and the family that he was leaving.

Suzy spent some time with his family, before hitting the streets to sow his seeds. As he approached Rosie's block, with a bottle of Hypnotic in his hand, he was excited. He ran to the building, up the stairs, and rang the doorbell.

"Yo, Rosie, open the fucking door, it's me!"

"Who?"

"Suzy!"

"How are you doing, Suzy? Nobody told me you were home!" She said letting him in, as a young couple walked out of the apartment.

"I'm cool. I've only been home a few hours. But I can see you still haven't changed," he said, with a hint of sarcasm in his voice.

"Don't even go there! They mean nothin' to me. I get what I want when I want and that's it." She was upset.

Although he was angry, the only thing that mattered to him was getting into Rosie's panties.

"Your crib is laced. Damn, girl! You getting paid."

Laughing, Rosie took the bottle of Hypnotic from him, seeing that he was already tipsy. He was so eager to fuck her, that he forgot about the glass of Hypnotic she poured for him. He pounced on her as he began removing both their clothes.

"Take it easy, baby!" Rosie said with a look of pain etched on her face as he forced his dick inside her.

"A'ight. Is this cool?"

"No!" she replied, spreading her legs wider.

"Like this?"

"Yeah, that's better!"

Suzy was tripping, trying to make up for the months he was away. He began banging Rosie's pussy from several positions, and within minutes he came.

"Damn!" Rosie said. "What were you trying to do, fuck out my pussy?"

"I ain't fuck in a minute. A brotha was feenin that's all."

"I can tell," she said, laughing. "Staying?"

"No doubt!"

Suzy was on a mission. He not only made the rounds with Rosie but with several other girls. He knew it was only a matter of time before he would be facing the judge. He was scared, yet he tried to downplay the seriousness of the charges he faced. He drank, smoked, and fucked every day as if it were his last. He did whatever it took to mask the uneasiness and apprehension he felt.

In November of 2004, his case went to trial. It lasted four weeks and the defense presented a stirring case. Suzy's top-caliber lawyers worked their asses off, respectively. However, the prosecution had insurmountable evidence and presented a strong case, and in the end, he was found guilty and given several life sentences. When asked by the judge if he had anything to say. He nonchalantly stood up and said, "Yes, your honor! Fuck you and the prosecutor! Fuck your mother and father! Fuck y'all!"

Then without hesitation, he bolted toward the judge who hauled ass into his chamber. The court officers immediately subdued him. His family and friends were shocked. Maria and his mother were in tears.

"Mami, I love you! Don't worry. I'll be okay," he said defiantly, as he was cuffed and then dragged into the back. Gone was his swagger!

When Black received word, that Suzy was sentenced and how he acted, he was saddened, but not surprised by his behavior. He was a ticking time bomb. Black felt bad for the family, especially Maria.

***

With the New Year about to take shape, Black decided to sit down with his police contacts. It was time for both sides to make some changes. He also decided to make several changes within the organization and in his business and private life.

One was allowing Maria to accompany him on his business trips. Initially, when he started doing business in the Midwest and southern states, those responsibilities belonged to Speedy and Blaze. Nevertheless, as the money started rolling in, it became more feasible for him to get actively involved.

Yet it was the constant pressure from Speedy and Blaze, who reminded him of how important it was for him to go and see how things were. They were the ones who talked him into expanding the business outside of New York City.

EPISODE 21

Love was in the air and Adiba's heart as she fell madly in love with a young man named Robert Mack. They met in the winter of 2004, and as they saw more of each other, Adiba felt he was her Mr. Right. Her family was happy for her, and the thought of being a wife and mother thrilled her as she wondered how she would handle her new life, along with law school.

An attractive young woman, she was light in complexion and a bit on the thick side. She stood an inch taller than her mother. Her hair was in a low-cut natural style that was stylish and elegant. A year younger than her brother, she was quiet and shy growing up. She was never the party type or in the streets. Her mother made sure of it. She spent the majority of her time at home, school, the library, and hanging out with her best friend. Robert Mack was smitten by her striking good looks as well as her intelligence.

In late June of 2005, Adiba and Robert were married. Black was supportive and happy for her. Robert Mack was several years older than Black. He was slim in build and stood six-three. Light in complexion with dark brown eyes, he was the proprietor of a car dealership, which was having its share of problems. Though he never graduated from college, he attended Howard University. A shrewd businessman, he was doing quite well until he made several questionable moves. And having Black as a brother-in-law would be rewarding, as well as a detriment.

Finding Black's business adventures appealing, Robert figured it would only be a matter of time before he would become a part of his close-knit inner circle. While Black and his entourage sat at a table in the VIP section of his restaurant one night, Robert couldn't help but notice the many guests who greeted him as he smiled, shook a few hands, and whispered in their ears. Robert's brain was working overtime as he approached his table and struck up a conversation. He was looking for a way to maintain his car dealership and he needed money, and he needed it fast.

Manipulative, deceptive, and always looking for a scapegoat or someone to take advantage of, Robert was well-schooled and versed in getting the things he needed to keep his business going. He loved Adiba, and he knew she felt the same way about him. Convincing her to put in a good word on his behalf to Black wouldn't be a difficult task.

Unaware of Robert's financial woes, Mrs. Reynolds was quite fond of him. He shared the same sentiment. Yet he had enough sense to know that trying to use Mrs. Reynolds to get closer to Black wasn't a good idea. He was close with other family members as well, but quickly realized he would be taking quite a risk if he mentioned a word about Black's business practice to them.

***

The streets were hot once again, despite the launch of several new police policies. The crews began crossing the imaginary lines which were agreed upon. The Jamaicans and the Asian dealers were terrorizing the neighborhood. The Jamaicans were moving a lot of highly potent marijuana and cocaine. It was lights out for anyone who got in their way. They controlled West One Hundred and Forty-Fifth Street and St. Nicholas Avenue.

People were shocked when they found out that the Asians were doing business in the neighborhood. They weren't selling their products from storefronts and apartment buildings or hanging out on the street corners. They plied their wares through their wholesale connection. They moved a lot of cheap dope with exotic names. The streets of Harlem were filled with it.

The Mexicans also got into the act. They were involved in dope, weed, crack, and cocaine. Although they sold to a largely Spanish clientele, they were making the rounds in Harlem by doing business with several African American, Jamaican, and African dealers. You name it, the Mexicans had it or they could get it for you. As well as cold-blooded killers, they knew the established dealers resented their rapid rise.

Death was a part of the business, and as the new and established drug gangs fought for their turfs, Black was livid. He didn't appreciate how the Asian and Mexican gangs were muscling their way into Harlem's underworld. They were making a lot of money, and he and Trigga wanted their share. They were paid top dollars by the Asian and

Mexican gangs to distribute their products in the "hood", yet they couldn't prevent the bloodshed from continuing.

The killings were raising a lot of eyebrows from law enforcement officials. Black's contact finally told him to calm things down. The carnage was too high for even Willie and his rogue partners. Black did his part, but he knew it was only a matter of time before things would explode once again. Within less than a week, after giving his word, four members of his crew were shot dead.

Trigga's crew fared no better as two of his partners were shot and hacked to death. Black and Trigga were on the case immediately. They weren't going to sit back and remain quiet. Not one stone was left unturned as the payback was astronomical. Bodies were found in abandoned buildings, cars, backyards, and alleyways.

"Yo, Black, we gotta get rid of these mutha- fuckas," Trigga said.

"Yeah, those niggas are acting up. We gotta do these poo-put, do-do scooper crews."

"Rude boy, we have to set mutha-fuckas straight, for real."

"That's why I'm here, son. I want you to do me a favor."

"What kind of favor?"

"I want you to take this mutha-fucka out for me. This punk took my money, and he ain't come through." He had a scowl on his face.

"Just get me the info, I got your back."

"For real, let's do this homie," he said, as they began discussing their plan.

***

Later that night . . .

"I thought we was supposed to do them mutha-fuckas, Coolio, and Hits?" Divine asked.

Black knew Divine was right, not that he had forgotten, but because of how things had played themselves out. He had to wait for things to settle down.

"True that. We'll do them tonight," Black said, waving his finger. "I know what I said before, but tonight I want y'all to roll with the rest of us."

It was 10:45 p.m., and it was a cool summer night. A thunderstorm had abruptly ended, leaving several puddles of water in the streets around East Eighth Street and Broadway. As the cool wind blew, several couples held hands as they made their way through Washington Square Park. Sitting at a table for three at Bar Banna, an exquisite bar and restaurant situated two blocks from New York University were Coolio, Hits, and an unknown man along with three beautiful, voluptuous women. Sitting across from the men were their two bodyguards.

A number of the dinner guests hadn't arrived as Bird and Speedy entered the restaurant. They were led to a table a few feet from the men. Bird was smiling at the bodyguard closest to her, and as he returned her smile, Black, Trigga, Divine, Infinite, and Riff, with masks on, and armed with several high-powered weapons, entered, and opened fire on the men. Coolio and Hits, along with the three women, were sprayed with a fusillade of bullets.

It was mayhem. It was chaos. The shooting lasted for a minute. Coolio was hit twelve times. Hits' bullet-riddled body was hit with fifteen rounds. The women were killed instantly. The bodyguards returned fire, hitting Infinite several times in the torso. Bird was hysterical as her brother fell mortally wounded. With tears streaming down her face, she crept up behind the bodyguard whom she had smiled at less than a minute ago and let loose with a barrage of bullets to his head.

The other bodyguard was also cut down. Breathing heavily, several of the restaurant-goers tried to help him. But they had to flee for their lives, as Black and Trigga opened fire on them. One of the men who tried to help the bodyguard somehow managed to make his escape during all the chaos. As they bolted from the restaurant, one of the diners, an off-duty correction officer, drew his weapon and announced himself. He was immediately cut down. Divine ran over to his body and blasted him in the forehead. Infinite was dead. Bird took one last glance at her brother's body before making her escape with the others.

"Is everyone else here?" Black asked.

"Yeah," they hollered, getting into the cars. Bee, Fats, and the other driver roared off with their tires screeching.

Back at the safe house . . .

"Damn! I'm so sorry, babes!" Black said to Bird. She rested her head on his chest. He tried comforting her, but she couldn't help herself as she began crying. Black was in a somber mood and so were the others. The only sound in the room was coming from Bird.

"They got him, Black! They got him!" she wailed. "What am I gonna tell my mother?"

He didn't know what to say. He had a worried look on his face as he mumbled, "You got to tell her. What else are you gonna say?"

"But I don't know how and where to start," she replied, wiping her face.

"Just tell her, that's all you can do."

"Okay," she barely, murmured.

"Don't worry about the expenses for the funeral. I'll take care of everything."

"Nah, Black, I got it," Divine said, as tears welled up in his eyes. "That was my dawg; I got this. It's the least I can do."

"No doubt," Speedy said, his voice also cracking.

The tears were flowing as Black, Trigga, Bee, and Fats tried their best to keep from crying. But the emotion was too much, as they got teary-eyed.

"This is for you, Lil Bro," Bird said as she pulled out her notebook and wrote in it.

"What's that?" Black asked.

"It's just my way of sending off my brother," she said to him between sniffles.

One week later, Infinite was given an official gangster's funeral and burial. With the funeral and burial behind him, Black knew he couldn't take a day off. The police were watching his every move and Hits partners were also on the prowl. Death loomed everywhere as he reflected on the myriads of killings his crew had participated in. However, he refused to acknowledge anything else but his survival and welfare. And in the words of "Downtown Slim," one of Harlem's original gangsters and most feared, Black remembered these words, 'Youngblood, my mama always told me that she would rather come and visit me in a jail cell, instead of putting me in a coffin before my time.' Those words had a lasting impression on him, because not only did Downtown Slim live a long life, but he also never spent any real time in jail other than to get processed at Central Booking and then later released.

EPISODE 22

Two weeks after the burial of Infinite, the tension between Black and Big Jeff had heightened beyond its boiling point. The streets were hot. The game was being played, and the players were ready. The door-die mentality was stepped up, and things were getting dangerous. It wasn't long before the two enemies crossed paths. Both men were in an after-hour spot owned by a businessman by the name of Denver Cannon, who went by the name, Uno. Denver was shot in his left eye during an armed robbery as a young man, hence the name.

The after-hour spot located at East One Hundred and Nineteenth Street and Lenox Avenue was filled with players, drug dealers, gamblers, prostitutes, and old-timers, you name it, and they were there. Speedy, who was with Black, spotted Big Jeff with two of his goons in one of the private gambling rooms.

Speedy thought about taking out Big Jeff himself but thought better of it, and instead told Black. Black knew this was his opportunity to get even.

"Black, we got that pussy cornered, let's do him!" Speedy said, his adrenalin rising.

Grabbing Speedy by his arm, he sternly whispered to him, "Come on now, you know that's not our style. That's not how we roll, we're gonna do this shit the right way. We're gonna wait for his ass outside, you feel me?"

"No doubt, I got you."

They were prepared. Their guns were drawn, when Big Jeff and his partners came strolling out of the after-hour spot.

"Yo, here they come!" Speedy said.

"Cool, wait for them to get in the middle of the street."

"A'ight."

Big Jeff was talking and laughing with his partners, unaware of his fate. Stuck in the side of his mouth was a cigar, as he and his boys walked toward his car. Black and Speedy struck from between two parked cars. Big Jeff and his boys reached for their weapons, but it was too late as they were hit repeatedly in their torsos. Big Jeff, hit the ground with a thud as the bullets ripped into his body.

"Fuck you, Black! Fuck you!" he managed to scream through blood-filled teeth, grimacing as he fired several rounds from his weapon, missing his intended target.

Within seconds all three men lay dying, Big Jeff tried to crawl his way back inside, but Black would have none of it. As Big Jeff slowly turned his head, he came face to face with Black and his Glock, as they stood over his blood-filled, cowering body. With blood pouring from the corner of his mouth, Black coldly stared into his eyes and said, "This is for Ray, mutha-fucka! And your boy, Shrug is next!" as he pumped several rounds into his forehead.

Big Jeff and his partners' bodies lay motionless in the blood-splattered street and on the sidewalk. Confident that there wasn't a witness to the bloodbath, Black remained at the scene as Speedy got in the car and sped off. Within minutes, the police and an ambulance arrived. After removing the bodies, the police closed down the after-hour spot.

Black calmly flagged a cab and left the scene. His confidence was sky-high, knowing that he remained at the scene and not one person looked at him suspiciously.

***

The news of Big Jeff's death hit the wire immediately. His adversaries and friends were stunned as to who would be bold enough to pull off such a hit, especially in front of Uno's place of business. Speculation was running rampant, and the police feared no better. The commissioner of police feared an all-out blood bath on the streets of Harlem.

Panamanian Shrug immediately took over as boss of the Webster Avenue crew. Easily voted in as the organization's new leader, he believed it was important for the members to remain calm. He felt they should channel their emotions elsewhere for the time being, and refrain from doing anything stupid.

"We know that mutha-fucka Black and his people did it. They ain't going nowhere, just chill, we'll get them. Those niggas got beef with everybody, including Coolio and Hits', homies. They'll fuck up, trust me, and when they do, we'll do 'em. They o'd'ing, but as I said, don't sweat it. We'll get our revenge." Shrug was confident as he spoke.

***

Three days later . . .

"Hey, Woody, Joey is wasted," Mike the bartender said.

"Yeah, I think I should take his drunken ass home."

"How come you didn't drink tonight, Woody?" Mike asked.

"You don't think two beers were enough?"

"Fuck no! That's what you look like most of the time," Mike laughed, pointing at him.

"Fuck you, shit head!" Woody said, grabbing ahold of Joey and heading out of Gallagher's Bar.

"See you tomorrow, Mike."

"You too, Woody, get home safe!"

Woody was driving south towards the Westside Highway when three motorcycles pulled up next to him. He looked at the men as their engines roared. He thought nothing of the three men as one of them did a wheelie on his motorcycle. Turning from the men, he began talking to Joey, when the men pulled out several hi-powered weapons and opened fire. Their bodies hit multiple times, jerked, and twisted like rag dolls before slumping onto each other as the car slammed into a parked trunk. William Woods, the white cop, and his black partner Joseph Green was taken out like players in the game. The three men then sped off into the darkness of the night.

“Yo, Black!” Riff called, as Black, Speedy, and Bee ate Kentucky Fried Chicken in the back room of the safe house.

“Waddup?”

“We just heard that Woody and his crimey, Joey got merked.”

“Hmm, those bitches had it coming to them. That’s what happens when you fuck with my shit and don’t keep your word,” he smirked.

“Who took them out?” Bee inquired.

“Who the fuck you think? Trigga!” Speedy said, smiling before Black could respond.

“This is our city, and we don’t give a fuck! I got to give him a call.” Black stated. As he reached for one of the many phones he used.

“Nice work,” he said to Trigga as the others looked on.

“Told you it was a done deal, son. This is how we live; one hand washes the other.”

“You done know, Trigga. Im’a call a meeting in a few days and see if these clowns wanna clear the air. I want you to be there. I wanna see if we can start a dialogue with some of these cats. I’m hoping they go for it.”

“Yeah, man, just link me.”

“Cool,” he said, hanging up the phone.

***

As promised, Black contacted several of the most important drug bosses for a sit-down meeting one week later. Trigga was there with several of his partners. The first thing Black did, was to remind the men that the Webster Avenue crew was still in effect, and their operations were being run by Panamanian Shrug. He tried his best with the help of

Trigga to get the Jamaican crew to the meeting, but they weren't interested. Black and the men spoke about respecting each other's boundaries and customers. Several of the men felt the new drug gangs were overstepping their boundaries and were rerouting the established crew's customers to their drug houses.

"This is exactly what I'm talking about!" Black snapped. "We have enough customers for every crew in this damn city. All we have to do is put aside our minor differences and stop being so jealous and greedy. If we do this, and I know we can, maybe we can stop a lot of the bullshit that's been going down." Several of the men nodded in agreement as he continued. "Shit is so good; we even have the mutha-fucking po-po eating out of our fucking hands. These mutha-fuckas are living lovely. They tell us when shit is going down, what more do we need? This is what it's all about! There's enough to feed the needy and the greedy if you know what I mean."

"But what about these young cats who think it's cool to fuck with our food?" a brother from one of the crew asked.

"Look, you do what you gotta do to set examples. What I'm talking about is the bullshit that keeps the po-po who ain't on our payrolls on our asses. These are the mutha-fuckas I'm talking about," Black said.

"I hear you," several of the men replied.

They agreed it was okay to sell whatever drugs they wanted. The bottom line was to respect each other. Finally, he told the others that the cops who were on their payroll must be aware of the boundary lines. And they must recognize and respect them also. He emphasized that if the guidelines, which were mutually agreed upon by all the crews in attendance were not followed, it would bring a lot of unnecessary heat and ultimately lead to all the crews' demise.

"Hey, if a dude taking food outta my mouth, he's gonna feel my steel," Trigga said.

"What the fuck he said?" One of the men asked.

"All he said was we work too hard to make our money, and for someone to come and fuck it up isn't cool," Black replied.

"Yeah, I hear you. I'm with that shit!" the boss of the Dirty Boys crew from Bradhurst Avenue said.

The meeting itself went relatively well, despite the mood of some of the men. Each crew knew what was expected of the other, and that was to go out and make the plan work.

For several months, things went well. But after a few setbacks and promises that were not kept, the violence started once again. Bodies were ending up in the coroner's office regularly, including innocent children and adults caught in their crossfire. Black, Trigga, and Divine were in the middle of the bloodbath. The crews were oblivious to everything and everyone. None of them gave a damn. Their total disregards for human lives were despicable, and their actions led to numerous arrest and deaths.

Some were given life sentences; others were murdered, and several drug houses were closed down. Despite his crew losses, Black was still a formidable opponent. In one particular incident, he had several of his foot soldiers dressed in police uniforms carry out a hit. He also had them dress in women's clothing to take out a rival in Hollis, Queens.

EPISODE 23

Divine entered the building. Standing in the lobby by the elevators were four thuggish-looking men with whom he was familiar with. He struck up a conversation with them, but he quickly became annoyed, because he was being searched.

"The shit is in the whip. Why the fuck y'all keep searching me, knowing I always leave my burner? Ain't that the mutha-fucking rules?" Divine snapped.

The men smiled as they completed the search. Only then did they allow him to get on the elevator. Two of the thugs got on the elevator with him. The elevator came to a stop on the sixth floor. The three men began walking down the hall. They approached apartment 6B. Divine chatted with one of the thugs.

"This is some tight security, son. Every time I roll up in here, y'all be putting a mutha-fucka through some new shit."

"You can never have enough security," the thug replied.

"I'm tired of going through this bullshit every time I do business with y'all."

"Nigga, if you feel like that then you shouldn't do business with us. Don't argue with me; argue with the big man inside. He makes all the rules," the other thug snapped, angered by Divine's ranting.

"Whaddup, Divine?" the brother asked, sitting in his leather lazy boy chair as he entered the room.

"I'm good, son, but what's up with your security? Every time I come here you put some new shit in place."

Laughing, he said, "It's better to be safe than sorry. My mama taught me that."

"Shit, you might as well put up some video cameras and monitors. And get rid of some of those niggas you have working."

"You a funny mutha-fucka," the brother said to Divine as both men laughed.

"You got that?"

"Yeah." Divine took the envelope and put it inside his shirt pocket.

"Say waddup to my homie Black for me."

"A'ight, son, see you next month."

As Divine approached his Benz, he noticed a group of men standing a few feet from it. He recognized several of them.

"Waddup, Divine? How is business?" One of the men hollered.

"Oh, shit!" Divine said. "Damn! You just the mutha-fucka I wanna see."

"Word?" the young man said.

"Yeah," Divine said, walking toward him. The two then walked a few feet to the side of one of the buildings.

He was about to tell the young man his reason for wanting to see him when a shadowy figure in a hooded sweater with his face concealed made his way through the group of men and pulled out a nine-millimeter Glock and aimed it at him. Fearing for his life, Divine made a run for it, but it was too late.

"Oh, shit!" he said aloud, as several bullets ripped into his body.

"Turn the fuck over bitch, so we can see your face!" the shadowy figure shouted. There was a look of shock and dismay on his face as the shadowy figure used his feet and turns him on his back.

"Who the fuck are you? What? What?" Divine muttered. Confused, delirious, and dazed, he tried his best to make out the voice of the shadowy figure.

"Mutha-fucka, you thought you would get away with that shit, huh? What's the trademark, bitch?" the shadowy figure screamed at him. "Look at this mutha-fucka, y'all!"

The group of men was now standing over Divine. The crowd parted, and there stood the man he had just visited in the apartment. Kneeling over Divine, he said, "I told you to say waddup to Black, didn't I? I guess he told you what's up, huh? You bitch ass mutha-fucka! How could you betray Black like that?"

Divine's eyes were rolling toward the back of his head. He had a wild look on his face, one of defiance, which quickly turned to one of regret. He believed it was Speedy concealing his face. He reached for his hand but got the shock of his life when he realized who it was.

"She told me, you fucking fool!" Black snarled as he removed the hoodie that had concealed his face. "You think you could play me like that? Mutha-fucka, what's the trademark?"

"One to the head," Speedy said, walking through the throng of men as Black fired a round in Divine's forehead.

It was over in a matter of seconds, as he pumped an additional three rounds into his body. The man whom he had visited then reached in his shirt pocket and removed the blood-soaked envelope filled with cash and handed it to Black. Divine's lifeless body was left at the foot of the concrete basement.

***

Later that night, Black, Trigga, and Speedy pretended as if they were hurt by Divine's death as they discussed it with Bird and other members of his crew. They took his death hard, especially Bird. Divine's funeral was held at Jericho Baptist Church in Harlem, a week later.

"Yo, y'all gotta go," Speedy said to Black and Trigga. "It ain't gonna look right if y'all don't show up. We grew up with the mutha-fucka, somebody gotta represent. That shit ain't gonna look right, mutha-fuckas might think we did the shit; you know what I'm saying?"

"I hear that, but what about you, you not coming?" Trigga asked him.

Before he could respond, Black said, "Don't worry about it. Trigga, me and you got it. For once that mutha-fucka is right."

Black and Trigga showed up at the funeral. The church was filled. Black wasn't aware that Divine knew so many people and had such a large family, despite being friends all those years. Both men slowly made their way to the white marble-closed casket. They touched the casket and walked to their seats.

As they observed the mourners, Black noticed Divine's mother and other family members; and waved at them. She coldly stared at both men. Black shrugged it off. *There is no way in the world she could have known that we merked him,* he thought to himself.

Black's eyes were fixed on Divine's mother and grandmother the whole time. And despite the tension, his face remained transfixed throughout the sermon. He never offered the family any money, nor did he offer his condolences. He felt there wasn't anything to verbalize as he looked on.

"Yo, let's bounce," Trigga exclaimed, clearly uneasy.

"Word! At least his bitch ass got a good send-off," Black snarled.

After the service, Divine's body was flown to North Carolina, where it was interred. Bird took over the leadership of his crew and did a really good job with the support of Black and Trigga. It didn't take long before animosity and jealousy amongst the members led to the organization reaching its low point and eventually its disbandment. Bird and several of her most loyal members joined the Syndicate.

***

One month later . . .

"What's up with that Moreno you introduced me to the day we went shopping?" Mercedes asked.

"Oh, him? Nada," Maria replied.

"Bitch, you lying. I've known you long enough to know when you lying. What happened? What about all that shit you told me?"

"Girl, a lot," Maria inhaled, taking a deep breath.

"Get the fuck outta here!"

"I'm serious, I ain't fronting. I fucked up," she replied in a regretful tone.

"What did you do, don't tell me you fucked that puta more than once?" Maria was silent for a minute before she began telling Mercedes what happened.

"Daag, Maria, what about Black?"

"At first I didn't give a damn about his feelings. He's been cheating on me since day one. So, I thought a little payback wasn't gonna hurt him."

"I can't believe this. You almost messed up your relationship. What if Black did all that fucking around? It still doesn't make it right, chica. Did you tell him?"

"No, I almost did."

"Wow! What did you say?"

"That I thought about it, but I couldn't go through with it. And I told him I saw the pictures."

"Damn! How did he take it?"

"He took that shit hard. He said he was sorry. And that he was going to keep it real with me from now on."

"Wow! You're fucking lucky he ain't beat your ass?"

"I know, but he was tight. I was crying my ass off. I was scared as shit."

"Are you gonna tell him?"

"Maybe one day, like years from now."

"Daag, Maria, you be playing some serious games. So that shit with you and that Moreno is over with, right?" It was obvious that Mercedes didn't know that Divine was dead.

"Yeah, it's over, but . . ."

"But what?"

"He got merked."

"Oh, my God! Black merked him?"

"Yeah, they clapped him up bad."

"See, I told you not to fuck with that mutha- fucka! You know how your man is. Mutha-fuckas be dumbing out behind shit like that, that's fucked up. I feel terrible."

"I know," Maria cried. "I'm so sorry; I don't know what I was thinking."

"When did this happen?"

"About a month ago."

"This shit happened a month ago, and you're just telling me. Damn, girl, what's up with that?"

"I know. I should have told you earlier."

"So how are things with y'all now?"

"It's cool, he watches my every move now, but he ain't got to worry about that anymore 'cause that's it for me. I am through with that stuff. He's been coming home and calling me more frequently than before."

"All this shit could have been avoided if you had just listened to me. Damn, that dude is dead for real, I can't believe that shit."

"I know. I fucked up. I should have listened to you. I think about that shit all the time."

"Just try and forget about that shit 'cause you can't do nothin' about it."

"I'm trying, but it's hard!"

"You crazy," Mercedes said, hugging her.

EPISODE 24

"Yo, Black, remember the Jamaica crew I was telling you about on White Plains Road?" Trigga asked.

"Yeah, son, what about them?"

"They got some wicked uncut Colombian they wanna get rid of."

"Word?"

"You done know."

"So, they willing to do business with you?"

"Yeah, son, it's on me."

The next day, Black and Trigga decided to visit the men. They were met by posse members Mikey, Fire, Pugs, and Spider.

"Yo, Mikey, do you have that thing?" Trigga asked.

"Yeah, man, it's here."

"How much are we talking about?"

"A hundred grand!"

"Cool. Then let's do business."

"Can I see what the product looks like?" Black asked.

"Fire, let him see the thing," Mikey said.

"Wait, this Yankee boy don't trust us. Cho, I don't like how this batty boy is looking at us," Fire said. He never got to say another word as three slugs hit him in the chest throwing him against the wall.

Black and Trigga quickly accosted the others before they could reach for their weapons.

"Why you shoot me? Bloodclaat!" he screamed, writhing in pain.

"You think I'm a faggot? Oh, me's a battyman? Because I look and talk this way you think I didn't understand you, fassy?" Black asked, with the hammer on his Glock pulled back.

"No, star, I didn't think none of that. I don't think you is a battyman," Fire cried out with a look of terror on his face.

"Battyman this, mutha-fucka!" Black snapped, blasting him in the forehead.

"The rest of you get down on the floor!" Trigga commanded. "Where the rest of the works and money at, fassy?"

"Is what this, Trigga?" Mikey pleaded.

"What you mean is what this? You don't have eyes? Wait, you an idiot? Shut your bloodclaat mouth and tell big man where the rest of the product is."

"You going to let us go once you get everything?" Mikey begged.

"Don't worry about it star, you safe," Black retorted, as he and Trigga nodded at each other.

After telling the men where the drugs and money were stashed, they put a bullet in each of their foreheads. Black and Trigga never meant any harm whatsoever. They came to conduct business until Fire's fatal mistake.

Speedy was beside himself when they got back to the car and told him what happened.

Laughing, he said, "Why y'all ain't call me?"

"We'll call you next time," Trigga said, snickering.

"Y'all look paranoid," he said, as the car sped off.

"Hmm," Black said. "You gotta have a certain mindset to do the shit we do. You should know that Speedy. This shit is like a chess match. A brotha can't afford to get checkmate. A mutha-fucka like me play to win every game."

"No doubt," Speedy responded.

"It's good to be paranoid because it prepares you for the unexpected and gives you an advantage," he continued. This was vintage Black, explaining how he stays one step ahead of his enemies.

"So Speedy, you never know this shit?" Trigga asked.

"Come on now. I don't wanna hear that shit."

"I keep telling him, Trigga, but he's getting there though," Black mockingly said as they all laughed.

"Remember this son, in the drug game, the ultimate rule is to be paranoid and never say never, 'cause anytime can be your time, believe me, rude boy," Trigga exclaimed.

As the car pulled up to a changing red light, Speedy nodded his head and said, "I'm feeling y'all," as the car slowly cruised along with the flowing traffic.

***

It wasn't long before the Internal Affairs, after an eighteen-month investigation, along with the cooperation of the Drug Enforcement

Agency and the City Task Force, cleaned out several precincts in Harlem and the Bronx. New commanders were brought in to run the precincts that were involved in the corruption fiasco. The high command at the central command center felt that to prevent morally good-natured cops from becoming corrupt, they had to get rid of the few bad apples, who had left a sour taste in the departments' mouths.

The officers involved included several detectives, patrol officers, and four captains. They were receiving monetary favors from several known drug dealers. They were fraternizing with convicted felons, which violated department policies. They were fired, arrested, convicted, and jailed. Not only was the high command incensed, the community leaders called for changes and the conviction of the officers who knew what was going on but chose to remain silent.

With many of his corrupted cohorts convicted and jailed, some of Black's adversaries were put out of business. Some were arrested and given lengthy prison terms. It wasn't like in the past, and rogue cops, dealers, informants, and numerous low-budget players had to think twice about getting involved with the real gangsters.

Black's affiliation with the neighborhood leaders and other influential persons within the Harlem community were growing more than ever. He was providing them with thousands of dollars, and he contributed mightily to their respective political campaigns. His businesses were also growing. He owned three supermarkets and two discount stores, a bar, two restaurants, and several apartment buildings along with his laundromats. Many of the respected folks within the community had no idea he was a high-level drug dealer and killer. The handful who knew kept quiet, as they feared for their lives.

Despite the rumors that he was the leader of a drug organization, people young and old gravitated toward him. He was aware of what was going on. Knowing this, he limited his participation in many of the events to which he was invited.

***

Adiba was doing well in her classes and couldn't keep her mind off Robert. The last time they spoke, he suggested she asked Black for a loan. She thought about it but then decided against it. Robert was furious, but his temper tantrum didn't last long. Instead, he began spending a lot of his free time at Stylz. Black didn't have a problem with him coming around. He didn't mind his friendship. He did notice that he was becoming familiar with several of his high-ranking members.

Yet, he felt that Robert's addition to his inner circle would be a positive, given his business savvy and experience. At the initial stage of meeting and hanging around Robert, he wasn't aware of the financial difficulties his dealership was going through. Nevertheless, when he was told, he asked Robert how much debt he was in.

"About a half a million," he said.

"What the fuck happened? How you owe so much paper? What's up with the bank?"

"I can't fuck with them. I fucked that up. Right now, I'm paying them back."

"Oh, you did, huh, and how much are you paying back?"

"I still owe them one hundred and seventy-five grand. I have to repay all that shit. So right now, I can't get a loan. You wanna know how I fucked up?"

"I'm listening."

"I pretty much got involved with some questionable characters when I first started the business. They lent me several thousand dollars with interest."

"Hmm."

"My whole thing was to double the amount they gave me once the business started showing a profit."

"You keep saying 'the money how much was it?"

"Three hundred and twenty-five thousand!" "Damn! You had to double that shit up and you fucked it up?"

"Yeah, man. I fucked it up! The bank gave me but so much paper. I had to go through a lot, Black, believe me. Now, these assholes wanna take over my business."

"It's not the bank you having problems with, right? It's your connection that's fucking you around?"

"Isn't that some shit, but I refuse to give it up. I have worked too hard. I'm not about to let them take my blood, sweat, and tears without a fight."

"Listen. I'll lend you the money and you do what you have to. Just make sure you pay me back my shit. 'Cause you don't wanna fuck with my paper."

"Black, you can count on that, believe me, you can."

"I'll have the money for you tomorrow."

"Can you do me a favor?"

"What's that?"

"Let's keep this between me and you. I don't want Adiba knowing anything about this."

"Don't worry about it."

The next day, Black gave the money to Robert, including an extra one hundred and fifty- grand. As promised, Robert used the money to pay off his debt. However, his former business partners were not satisfied. They were still demanding a share in the car dealership and Robert was as adamant as ever.

"Hell, no! This is my shit! You got your money. Now get the fuck outta here!" he yelled to his bald former partner.

"Nigga, you must be crazy! You have two fucking weeks to think this shit over or else," the bald brother replied, as he smashed Robert in the back of his head with his Colt Patriot .45.

With blood gushing from his wound, they stomped him as he fell to the floor. Scared, he tried to defend himself.

"Get the fuck up, nigga! Get up, bitch! Two weeks, that's it!" the bald guy reiterated.

"Okay, man," Robert said, getting up.

One of the men pulled a gun and fired three rounds over his head. Believing he was hit; Robert fell to the floor where he remained until the men drove off. Seeing he wasn't hurt, he rose to his feet, closed the dealership, and left. He immediately told Black about his confrontation with his former buddies.

"Don't worry about it," Black reassured him.

"Are you sure, man?"

"Yeah, I'm sure!"

"Those cats are vicious."

"I know. I said don't worry about it. All you have to do is follow my lead."

"Okay."

***

The day before the deadline, Robert got a surprise visit. He was about to close the dealership when two cars drove up and several tough-looking thugs got out and started smashing the windshields of several cars. He pleaded for them to stop. When they finally did, they began pistol-whipping him. Robert, pleading for his life, screamed and pissed all over himself.

"One more day, you hear me, mutha-fucka? That's all you have left. One more fucking day, and if it's not a done deal, your ass is ours," the pissed-off bald brother said. Instead of going home that night, Robert headed straight to Black's restaurant.

"What the fuck happen to you?" he asked, seeing the welts on his face.

"It's them niggas, man. I told you they're vicious."

"Hmm, we'll see about that!" he snarled.

Robert opened his business as usual the next day. He was pacing back and forth for most of the day. He was either going to give half his business to his former associates or stand up and fight as they drove up.

As a nervous Robert led his former buddies into his office, waiting inside were Black, Speedy, Bird, and Riff. Realizing they had walked into a trap, the four men tried to make a run for it. Robert quickly slammed the door shut on them. Staring at four twelve-gauge shotguns, the men began pleading as Riff disarmed them. They were led from the office to a back staircase, which leads to a storage room, where they were tied and blindfolded.

It was dark outside. They were led to their cars and driven to a wooded section off the Southern State Parkway on Long Island. Taken from the trunk of the cars they were shoved face down in the dirt.

"You niggas like to fuck with people's shit, huh? Y'all got paid, but still wanted more. Y'all ain't nothin' but a bunch a greedy mutha-fuckas!" Black snapped.

"Yeah, mutha-fuckas, I warned y'all," Robert added.

Seeing he was hyped and ready to take care of business, Black called him over, "Yo, put a bullet in this mutha-fucka's head."

"Huh?"

"I said put a bullet in this mutha-fucka's head."

The look on his face quickly changed from one of excitement to horror. His nerves were getting the best of him as he stood there shaking in fear. He was stuttering. Black couldn't believe what he was seeing as he stared at the others in disbelief.

"What? You want me to shoot him?" he stammered.

"No, I want you to give that bald nigga a haircut," Black snapped.

"Okay, okay! But I don't wanna use that," he said.

"Shoot that mutha-fucka!" Black commanded in a cold tone.

"Give me that one," he said, sheepishly pointing at the forty-five automatic in Black's waistband.

"This nigga is a bitch-ass!" Speedy declared.

"He's stuttering like a little bitch!" Riff added.

"Bitch? This mutha-fucka is worse than a bitch," Bird smirked.

Taking the forty-five from his waistband, Black handed it to Robert. He placed the nozzle of the gun against the head of the bald brother. He nervously stared at Black before pulling the trigger. The noise echoed in the night. Six more rounds were fired in succession into the heads of the other three men. Robert couldn't bear to look at the lifeless bodies as Black snatched his weapon from his hand. His cold, deep, and dark piercing eyes cut into Robert like a sharp blade. He remained quiet as he considered his next move.

Upon hearing about the death of their partners, Robert's former business associates vowed revenge. However, they soon realized that Robert was no longer involved with the dealership. Black took it over, sold it within two months, and split the money with him. Robert relocated to Westchester, where he opened a new dealership. Black knew Robert was quite the character, and he wondered how he would fare under the intense pressure, knowing that he had committed a murder. Yet, Black remained optimistic that he wouldn't go to the police.

EPISODE 25

The year was coming to an end, and with some reservations, Black made his appearance at the Manhattan criminal court. With a reserved look on his face, he stared straight ahead as his lawyers spoke. Tried as they did, they couldn't get the charge dismissed. He was given five years' probation for possession of a deadly weapon. He was cool about the whole thing. He thought his court appearance went smoothly as he left court with a pregnant Maria on his arm.

He certainly didn't like how the year ended. Yet, he was extremely optimistic as he looked forward to the New Year. Maria gave birth to healthy twin girls, and he was elated. He was happy with the newest members of his family. He was spending more time at home helping out with the twins. Despite the happy home outlook, Maria knew he was still seeing other women, including Bird. There were rumors about him fathering other children, which he did, but he was smart enough not to bring them around her.

Although Maria was familiar with Yvette, she wasn't pleased knowing they had a child. But this was something she had to deal with. No one and I mean no one was going to come between him and his children. As upset as she was, she knew that he took care of his children. He lived up to all the obligations of being a father. Money wasn't an issue when it came to the children and their mothers. He took time out of his busy schedule to visit and spend time with them.

He and Maria had spoken on several occasions about putting up the house for sale and relocating to Florida.

"I'm seriously thinking about making that move, babes," he said to her one night.

"What move?"

"Remember, we spoke about it just last week."

"You mean, Divine?"

"Nah, that's old news, baby. Forget about it, ma. The best thing you ever did was tell me. Me and you have been through a lot. Ain't nothin' gonna stop this. It's over with, so let's put it behind us, okay?"

"Okay."

"Are you ready to make that move? I ain't gonna ask you again because we spoke about it."

"We spoke about a lot of stuff last week. Oh, shit! You mean, Florida?"

"Hell, yeah, that's what I'm talking about."

"Are you serious, baby?"

"Yes, I am," he said, hugging her.

***

The Syndicate still had some unfinished business to take care of given the setbacks suffered in the South and Midwest. The continued killing of his workers and the loss of large quantities of drugs were not encouraging. Black knew he wasn't the "man" so to speak in those states. But he knew he had made a mark, and despite the danger, the crew was still making lots of money.

These were some of the issues that worried him, and after talking it over with his rank and file and those closest to him, he decided he would leave the garden state for the sunshine state at some point during the year. He also put into motion the changes he had promised. Within four months, he and Maria were shuttling back and forth from New York to Florida, North Carolina, Virginia, Connecticut, and Ohio.

The drug war between the local crews and the gangs from New York was weighing heavily on him. The local dealers were pissed because the New Yorkers had moved in on their turfs. They didn't give a damn, as their dislike for the New Yorkers grew.

The locals knew how ruthless and vicious they can be. There was an unwritten rule about New Yorkers, and that was whenever you're in a confrontation with any of them, "do them first and save the lip service."

Taking out a dealer from New York was like a badge of honor. The majority of brothers that did business out of state, especially in the south and Midwest were there to build their cash flow.

The drug flight to the south was about money. Black and his crew brought drugs, violence, and death, unlike anything they had ever seen. Crews from the south and Midwest hardly ever conducted their business on the east coast. Every drug dealer on the east coast knew that the streets of the Midwest and the south were paved with "dead presidents".

***

Quite a few influential people within the business community began questioning the legality of Black's legitimate businesses. There were rumors that his lawyers were laundering thousands of dollars from his illegal activities through his legitimate businesses. And several merchants in the community were involved. When news of this got back to Black, he immediately started a ghetto public relations campaign to downplay the whole thing.

"You see what I'm talking about?" he said to Speedy, one afternoon.

"Yeah, that's fucked up. These people never mind their fucking business. They always in somebody's shit."

"Now these mutha-fuckas are saying that I'm laundering my paper through my legit businesses here in Harlem. Now I've got to talk to my lawyers, and also hit the streets like I'm some fucking politician."

"Why you gotta hit the streets? I don't get it?"

"I gotta let my legit business partners know what's going down. They haven't heard anything from the wire. I've got to update them."

"No doubt. Yeah, that's a good idea."

"Plus, I've got to hit some of these bitches with a few grand to keep them cool, you feel me?"

"No doubt."

Black then headed home and told Maria about the things being said about him and his business associates.

"Just do what you need to do, that's all," she said in a comforting voice.

"That's why I fucks with you." He smiled.

***

Despite the controversies concerning his personal life and the changes he talked about, Black decided to visit Bird.

"We need to talk," he said to her.

"About what?"

"Hmm."

"I hate when you do that 'hmm' shit, Black."

"Come on now, I'm serious."

"I'm serious too."

"This is what's up, I'm thinking about moving my family to Florida. Let me rephrase that, I'm moving my family there."

"I knew something was up, but if that's what you gotta do. Then go ahead and do you."

"I'll still be around. It's not like I won't be here."

"Whatever, Black, it's your loss anyway, and you the one who'll be missing this!"

"It won't be nobody's loss, I ain't leaving you. I ain't going nowhere, you think I'm gonna leave this pussy?"

"I don't know. Are you?"

"I'm not, what about you?"

"What about me?"

"Are you gonna leave this dick?"

"No comment," she said, smiling.

"Look, it's gonna be all good. Do you believe what I'm saying to you?"

"Yeah. I believe you."

He pulled her close and kissed her. The heat in the room soared. She quickly loosened his pants and began sucking his manhood.

"Don't suck it so hard!" he moaned.

"If you leave, this is what you'll be missing," she said, wrapping her lips around his dick and began driving him crazy. Their lovemaking that night was incredible — they fucked for hours.

EPISODE 26

Black was comfortable with some of the decisions he had made, as he and Maria spoke. He felt he had a new lease on life. He began questioning his lifestyle. He didn't seem as attached to the streets as he did in the past. The doubts were creeping in as he was spending more time at home than with his Syndicate family, including Bird.

"It took me a while to come to my senses, but I'm ready now. I lost a lot of people and did a lot of shit, things that I'm not happy about. I can't keep going on like this. If I were to die right now, I would be an unhappy man, because I wouldn't have done enough for you and the kids."

"Dante, please don't say these things."

"I have been talking a lot to my business partner in Brooklyn, and the more we talk, the more sense it makes for me to get out of the game."

"Dante, we're in a position to better our lives now. We have a family. You are doing the right thing baby; you're not that young impressionable kid anymore. You're a family man now."

Smiling, he said, "You're right, Maria; I have to be more than a gangster for my kids. I have to be a husband and father. Plus, my mom will be happy."

"She will," Maria said, squeezing his hand. "Are you sure you won't go back to your former lifestyle?"

"I'm sure, baby!"

"Okay, because it would disappoint a lot of people."

"I know," he calmly said.

***

Within weeks, a realtor was on the case, and their house was up for sale. His lawyers were also in the process of finalizing his transfer to Florida with the New York City Probationary Department. In a matter of days, the necessary paperwork was completed, and the transfer was approved. He and Maria bought a modest home in South Beach. They were living the good life in sunny Florida, chilling and sipping on Cristal, Clos Du Mesnil, and Krug. He fished, played golf, and even tried to surf. He was surrounded by family and friends as he looked forward to a wonderful life with Maria.

As he reflected on the many friends he lost along the way, he thought about his mortality. He knew if it weren't for the constant pressure from his mother and Maria, he would have remained in Harlem. The killings, the betrayals, the distrust, the corrupt rogue officers, the local politicians who knew he was a killer, yet willingly took his money, and his promiscuous behavior weighed heavy on his heart. Nonetheless, he felt that moving to Florida provided him with some sense of semblance. He felt that the others were capable of operating and maintaining the operations.

Aware that Speedy and Riff would have to work in tandem, to maintain the daily operation of the business in his absence; he felt confident that they would do a good job, or so he thought.

The operation was running smoothly. Speedy knew the daily nuances of the drug game and being in charge was something he had always looked forward to doing. Still, he had thoughts about striking out on his own. However, the bond that he and Black shared was built on trust and loyalty, and that meant a lot to him. Also, he didn't want to follow in Divine's footsteps. More than ever, he wanted to impress Black, and he did just that. He didn't have any favorites amongst the members, nor did he put up with any nonsense.

Riff was his second in command. He informed Black of all transactions, including several beat-downs, which he dished out himself on a few undesirables.

Black was in the third month of his so-called semi-retirement when he was told that Robert was constantly trying to undermine Speedy and Riff's authority. When Robert began acting up, Speedy and Riff wanted to take him out; but they knew they needed Black's permission. He was also giving Bird a difficult time, whenever she questioned his behavior. They were also worried about Adiba; they didn't want to hurt her by killing her husband. So, they decided to let Black know how they felt. He contacted Robert and told him to slow down and take things easy. He listened, gave his word, and assured him that he would.

That night as Black lay in bed his mind was on Adiba. He turned and looked at a sleeping Maria before checking on the children and returning to bed. Would he sit idly by and leave his brother-in-law at the mercy of his partners; which would devastate Adiba and his mother? Or will he head back to the dark underworld and streets of Harlem USA?

www.ingramcontent.com/pod-product-compliance
Lightning Source LLC
Chambersburg PA
CBHW070119260626
47160CB00004B/1538
9780615626093